The Surfer Alone

A Quiver of Surf Stories

by

Nick Bruechle

Contact the author:
www.nickbruechle.com
nick@nickbruechle.com
facebook.com/nickbruechlebooks
@nick_bruechle

ISBN 978-0-6450839-2-7
Set in Adobe Garamond Pro

To everyone who loves the ocean.

CONTENTS

I am swell

I was born in a storm. Of a storm. In the cold, turbulent re-gion at the base of the world, the barometric pressure fell so low that the air itself tried to lift the ocean up into the sky. My first peak arose there. Was built, boosted and directed by the winds that rush and harry, and ultimately command the desperate sea.

My existence is energy, my destiny is growth, my life is movement. When the growth stops, when movement ceases, my energy will dissipate as magically as it appeared, and I will be gone forever.

From the first, my life had but one objective: the islands of Indonesia. As I travelled, I grew and spread, radiating outward in a giant, perfect arc from the place of my birth. My objective did not change, but my reach widened.

As my heart sped north, my fingers brushed the limestone shores of Western Australia, touching a thousand islands and spending some small fraction of my energy on beaches and reefs along its green, white and red coast.

The waters through which I travelled grew warmer, clearer and brighter, and still I pressed on. Consuming the smaller and slower of my siblings, those that could not escape before me, absorbing their energy, I grew stronger, straighter. As the winds about me lightened, I gained discipline and order. Thus I reached my final destination pure and powerful.

As I surged those last hours to my demise, in many places I met reefs that gave my inherent energy explosive new shape and form.

On the morning of my last day, I first impacted the coast of Java, bringing barrels to its many ridden and hidden waves, from Pulau Panaitan to Grajagan. As the day grew older, I brought joy, frustration, terror and serenity to surfers in Bali, Lombok, Sumbawa and beyond. My power core intersected with the islands of the Mentawai chain, and it is there that I delivered the highest intensity of emotion and physicality. But still I was not done. My remnants travelled on, through the Banyak and Telo Islands, to Nias and beyond. At the end of my last day, I gave the last of my dying energy to the warm, brownish waters of Sri Lanka.

I had been to the furthest reaches of my ocean. Surfers had tasted of my energy briefly, ephemerally. Some will remember me all of their lives, others let me pass beneath them without a second thought. Others still cursed me for the fear I brought them or the damage I wrought them.

It's all one to me. I am swell.

Balangan 1974

The day was just beginning, but it was already hot, close and very still. The ocean was a sheet of burnished blue silver with long, straight lines of swell streaming into the bay in regular regimentation. Away over the empty space between Kuta and Benoa Harbour, the sun was creeping into the sky, a flaming ball of gold and heat. Kodok had already been to the base of the cliff, to the *pura* by the beach to place an offering, and now he was on his way home.

Standing at the bottom of the ragged wall towering above him he thought again of the day that he'd fallen down that very cliff. He'd been placing an offering that day too, but it hadn't saved him. He looked at his misshapen leg and then back up at the cliff. There was nothing he could do now. He sighed and began the climb.

He was expected at the *warung* soon, but there was still plenty of time for breakfast and the long, hot walk to work. He was now well used to his loping, bouncing gait, and although watching him made some people wince, he felt no real discomfort. Apart, of course, from embarrassment at their expressions, or the uneasy laugh that slipped out when they heard his nickname, *Kodok*, which means frog.

As he reached the cliff top, he was momentarily blinded by the rising sun, its rays striking him straight on as he came over the crown. He blinked and stared in wonder at the vision before him.

As he would later say to Made, 'I thought for a moment I was dreaming. There was a man walking towards me with the sun behind him, but he didn't look like any man I have ever seen. He looked like *Varuna*.'

Made, who never mocked Kodok, or offended him in any way, said nothing. She nodded for him to go on.

'He was tall, and with the sun behind him his skin looked like beaten gold, much lighter in colour than yours or mine, and it was covered with fine white hairs. The hair on his head grew well past his shoulders, dropping in waves and curls, and it was gold too.' Made's eyes widened.

'Was it just a trick of the light?' she asked. 'Did you blink?'

'Oh, I blinked,' said Kodok. 'And when I opened my eyes he was still there, only closer to me. Tall and powerful, with thick, bulging muscles, completely naked except for a pair of shorts covering him from here to here.' He indicated a small area from his hip line to just below his crotch. 'But the most amazing thing, the thing that made me wonder if he really was *Varuna*, was his weapon; his *Varunastra*.'

Varuna was the Hindu god of water, the ocean of stars above and the underwater realm, and it was said that his

Varunastra could assume any shape, like water. Only the skilled could use the *Varunastra*, and if the inexperienced tried to wield it they could be injured or killed. *Varuna* was special to Kodok because once, not long after his accident, his uncle Kadek had said that he had spoken to *Varuna*, and He had said that in spite of Kodok's mangled leg, the boy would do well in life, and that 'the ocean will be his source'.

Made wasn't feigning interest now, and she had adopted the same expression of excited gravity as her cousin. 'His *Varunastra*?' she said.

'His *Varunastra*,' he repeated solemnly. 'Shaped as a giant spear, as tall as a man, and wider than you. But it wasn't really a whole spear, because it had no shaft, it was more like a huge spearhead, with a tip that was shaped to a fine, sharp point. At the blunt end, which was still quite sharp, there was a fin just like half the tail of a tuna, sticking straight out of it sideways. The man held this giant spearhead lightly under his arm, like it weighed nothing.'

'What did you do?'

'I shielded my eyes and looked as hard as I could. I saw that there was another man with him, and this man was shorter, with dark hair and pink skin, but he was also carrying a spearhead like the other one. And they were coming towards me.

'I wondered if it was another one of *Varuna's* tricks, and I wanted to run away, but before I could, they saw me. I couldn't move. It was as though I was tied to the spot. They were both shouting and laughing in a way that made me think they weren't gods at all. They were very excited and they kept on pointing at the ocean, going "oooh" and "aaaah" every time a wave broke. The tall one said something to me, but I couldn't understand him. I think he was speaking English. They seemed very friendly, and from the way they were gesturing I guessed they wanted to go to the bottom of the cliff. I showed them the way, and when we got to the beach they dropped everything and ran into the water with their spears. They laid the spears flat on the water, with the tuna fin facing the bottom, and then they lay on the spears themselves, and they floated.'

Made was fascinated. She held her hands tightly together and leaned in closely to her cousin, keen not to miss a word. She'd grown up a lot in the last seven years – they both had – and she was now definitely becoming a young woman. Her face was a little longer but still beautifully proportioned, her neck and arms were slender and strong, and budding breasts were growing on her bare chest.

Kodok, rapt in his story, noticed none of this. It was perfectly natural for her to be dressed that way, the same as all the women in their village.

As he spoke, he had the look of someone who was having trouble believing the evidence of his own eyes, and he was a little breathless, as though reliving the scene as he retold it. 'And if that wasn't enough, they paddled their spears all the way out through the waves using only their arms, until they were beyond the reef. And then…' He passed his hands before his eyes. 'And then the tall one aimed his spear at the beach, and a wave came along and picked him up.'

Made was horrified. She clapped a hand to her mouth, anticipating the gruesome detail that would surely come, the awful story of the man being smashed into the coral. 'Ohhh,' she said.

'But instead of crashing head first into the reef,' said Kodok, 'he stood up straight on his spear, and made it glide across the face of the wave.'

'No,' breathed Made. 'How could he do that?'

'I have no idea,' said Kodok. 'But it wasn't an accident, because I watched him do it again and again and again, and the other man did it a lot of times too.'

'And that's what made you late for work?' cut in a strong, masculine voice. Made's father and Kodok's boss, Uncle Wayan.

'Yes uncle,' said Kodok. 'I'm sorry I was late, but it's true, every word of it. I'm not the only one who saw them, either.'

'Oh don't worry, I believe you,' said Wayan. 'I've heard of it. It's called surfing' – he used the Indonesian word *mainski* – 'and they've been doing it under the cliffs at *Uluwatu*, at the end of the *bukit* for some time now. I wondered whether our waves here would attract them.'

'The way they were carrying on, and their haste to drop everything to run into the water, I think they do,' said Kodok. He nodded sagely.

'Well, enough of that,' said Wayan. 'You're late and we have work to do. Begin by unpacking those cartons of cooking oil.'

Made carried the first box to the shelf, and Kodok helped her unpack and stack it. Kodok's mind was clearly not on the job; he would place the bottles with their labels facing the wrong way, or absently hold out his hand for the next bottle without noticing that he'd moved too far away for her to reach him from where she was sitting. She had to get up, sighing, and hand him the bottle.

All morning he fidgeted, and kept looking at the road to the beach to see if the surfers were coming back. He didn't pay attention to their daily reading lesson, and he got annoyed when Made asked him questions or tried to engage him with games or talk. Eventually, before retiring for his afternoon *istirahat*, or rest, Uncle Wayan said, not unkindly, 'you're not really here, are you Kodok? You can go now, and chase your crazy surfers.'

Kodok didn't need a second invitation – he was off hopping down the road as fast as his legs would carry him.

He found the surfers lying on the beach next to their big spear-shaped surfboards, attended by a small crowd of local children, and Uncle Kadek, who sat there cross-legged, smiling. The two white men chatted with each other, and the local kids all prattled and gawked shamelessly. Kodok joined the little throng, smiling broadly at the two surfers, and waited for something to happen.

The breeze off the land had strengthened by mid-afternoon, and great plumes of white spray were being blown off the tops of the waves as they rose, feathered and crashed with a mighty 'whump'. The swell had risen since the morning, and endless lines of surging ocean power were stacked to the horizon. When these met the reef, they broke with ruler-edged precision from the western end of the bay, under the headland massif, towards the Hindu temple – the *pura* at the rocky eastern end. The sound was like continuous rolling thunder, and the waves looked dangerously frightening.

The *desa* kids were full of talk about the brave gymnastics of these two strange, brave men through the morning. They had been able to stay just ahead of the breaking curl of the wave, standing tall on their surfboards as the ocean boiled and crashed around them. 'Sometimes,' said Agung, a boy a year younger than Kodok, 'they would squat down on their haunches and let the curtain of the wave fall over them so they were *inside* the wave. It was unbelievable.'

'I wish I had seen that,' said Kodok. Agung told him that the two had been fearless in the fierce waters, pushing through huge walls of angry foam to paddle back out through the breakers, occasionally taking spectacular falls from the very top of some of the waves into water just inches deep, only to come up smiling and laughing.

Kodok stole closer to the two relaxed, smiling surfers. He was about to reach out and touch one of the surfboards when the taller, blonde one of the pair stood up and dusted the fine white beach sand off his floral-patterned shorts.

'Time to go Ratty,' he said, and picked up the surfboard next to Kodok. He grinned at the boy and gave him the thumbs up, and Kodok returned the gesture with a toothy smile.

The smaller, darker man picked up his surfboard, a blazing yellow craft with the image of an impossibly round, hollow wave painted on its bottom, and the surfers ran to the water's edge.

The tide was fully out now, and the reef was exposed to the air for almost seventy metres; further down towards the headland local women were picking for oysters, mussels and tiny crabs, or harvesting seaweed from the communal plots.

The two surfers carefully picked their way out across the reef, and when the water they stood in was waist deep, they threw themselves at an oncoming wall of foam, expertly leapt onto their surfboards, and paddled out to meet the rising waves. Kodok was alarmed by the size and consistency of the waves, and the raw power of them. He need not have worried.

For the next two hours the little knot of children, growing

to include more than a few men, watched the two surfers take on the green, backlit waves. To those watching, the surf was huge and the act of being out there utter madness, and they were fascinated and terrified in equal measure.

Every new wave that arrived in the bay seemed to stand up taller and more menacing than the last, advancing in stately silence and growing even higher before throwing itself forward in one last graceful arcing surge. Many broke as hollow tunnels of water that sometimes spat misty cannonballs of spray out of their coconut-round mouths. And in the midst of this beautiful mayhem, the two surfers rode the deadly tubes with majestic confidence.

The tall blonde one was the most accomplished and assured of the two. He would stroke quickly but without any apparent effort, head down and feet kicking, until the wave picked up the tail of his board and carried it on its own momentum. At exactly the right juncture, he would jump to his feet with easy agility, almost faster than the eyes on the beach could track his motion.

Straight down the steep face he would streak, and as the speeding surfboard reached the trough, he would lean precipitously to his left, his whole body erect, and the board would magically turn to run parallel with the wave, throwing sheets of water as it spun. The surfer would then crouch, pointing the nose of the surfboard very slightly up, so that he seemed to be climbing slowly back up the face.

On some waves he crept forward on the board, which increased his speed relative to that of the wave, and stayed well ahead of the hollow part. But on most he slipped behind the crystal curtain of falling water and the people on the beach could just make out his silhouette, travelling at silken speed inside the bowels of the wave, before he disappeared and his board shot out of the foam. On one or two waves he even emerged from his watery cocoon to stand up straight and throw exultant arms to the sky before kicking out. On these waves the *ooohs* and *aaaaahs* of the crowd gave way to gasps and instinctive shouts of encouragement.

The other man went into some tubing barrels, but never did he emerge. More often he stayed well ahead of the hollow part, weaving his spear-like craft up and down in mesmerising rhythm, covering vast distances across the bay.

Every now and then he would be so far ahead of the curling part of the wave that he could press his left heel into the tail of the board to bring its nose almost all the way around to face back where it had just come from in an elegant half-circle, a great shower of spray cascading off the rail of the board all the way through the turn. Just when it seemed that he would ram head first into the rushing whitewater speeding towards him, he would carve another swooping turn and race ahead of the breaking part again.

The spectators were enthralled. They clapped. They cheered. They covered their eyes in horror and threw their arms in the air in triumph. It was without any doubt, judging from the shining eyes and admiring comments, the most astounding thing any, young or old, had ever seen.

Kodok sat in stunned disbelief on the beach, the animation of his features and his ever changing expressions of fear, joy, wonder and astonishment mirroring those of his fellow watchers. He and Agung, who sat – or more often stood – beside him looked at each other with mouths agape and eyes wide, and screamed, howled, laughed or just breathed in incredulous silence.

The sun was falling towards the horizon when the two surfers at last walked away from the water to the boisterous accolades of the gathered crowd. Almost everyone who lived within walking distance of the beach had heard of the exhibition in progress and made their way to the beach or clifftop to watch. A mob of over thirty was there to congratulate the surfers, many of the men patting them on the shoulders as they walked past, laughing.

They planted their surfboards in the sand, fins pointing towards the setting sun, and sat on the sand to catch their breath. Most of the adults, sensing that the show was over, drifted away. After a short while so did most of the children. But Kodok and Agung and a handful of others stayed close, watching the surfers' every move and snatching sideways glances at the craft they rode. These shining water-spears were intriguing – glossy, hard and colourful, and carved in the most alluring curves they'd ever seen. What they were made of and how they achieved the feats performed on them were impenetrable mysteries, and the *anak-anak* were entranced.

After a ten minute rest, during which the visitors spoke to each other in what Kodok became sure was English, having heard enough of it to be certain, the taller one stood up and his companion followed suit. The tall blonde god was about to pick up his surfboard when he saw just how intently Kodok was looking at it.

'You want to carry my board?' he said to the boy. Kodok looked at him, smiling but uncomprehending. 'You,' said the man, pointing at Kodok. 'Carry. My. Board.' He mimicked the action of picking it up and putting it on his head, and pointed back at Kodok. The lad understood that well enough, and in a flash he was on his feet, grabbing the surfboard and resting it on his head, marvelling at how light and shiny it was. He was off, loping up the beach towards the cliff before the surfer knew what was happening. Seeing the boy's limp, he ran after him and stopped him. 'Whoa little man, you gonna be alright with that?' he said. Kodok didn't know what was said but he'd caught the tone well enough. He'd heard it many times before. He gave the man a thumbs up accompanied by a cheesy grin. The other surfer allowed Agung to carry his board, and the four climbed the steep cliff path attended by a gaggle of giggling kids.

Kodok and Agung carried the boards all the way to Uncle Wayan's *warung*, where the men stopped to buy a drink, and then they disappeared into the gathering dark. As he watched them go, Kodok hoped with all his might that they'd be back.

He needn't have worried.

2004

Looking out from the door of his busy beachside *warung*, Kodok counted the black dots floating and paddling around the wide bay of Balangan. Some thirty hungry, thirsty and rich foreigners crowded the waves, and there were more arriving all the time. He thought back to that day, so many years before when Lee and Ratty had first come into the bay, and the magic they had weaved. Thanks to these surfers, he was now a well-to-do *warung* owner and respected village senior. Uncle Kadek had been right after all; the ocean was and would always be his source.

The Barrel

The day felt strong. He felt strong. Striding through the gilded October afternoon sunshine, his sense of power growing with every step.

'It should be pumping. There's a light onshore, but there should still be plenty of shape. If the swell from this morning is still there.'

He'd seen it early that morning, flashing past outside the tinted windows of his mother's car as she'd driven him to school. A straight westerly swell, the remnants of an almighty storm that had raged across the whole of last week.

A ragged, broken, lumpy, wind-torn swell that was hard to be in and harder to be away from had beaten onto the beach near his home every day for a solid week. And every day of that rain-sodden, windswept devil of a week, he'd made the tantalising trip past the swollen ocean to school, to sit exams. To wrack his brains, wresting out twelve years of learning in a few pressurised hours, in a sweat-stinking gym.

And in between to bury his head in books, his throat as dry as the pages he turned, imagining each to be a perfect barrel as he curled it over in his hands.

On this, the day of his last exam, the sun had ridden over a thin band of cloud in the east at dawn and leapt into a clear sky. The swell had straightened and become organised into regimented blue corduroy lines marching across the ocean.

He could see it as clearly as day, as his mother had driven him those long, last miles for that last exam. His last ever exam. That final moment of schooling for a lifetime. The long awaited portal into adulthood.

And now the exam was over. The door out of childhood had closed behind him and he was free. Literally free, and feeling strong.

When he got to the hilltop overlooking the beach, not a hundred metres from his house, he broke into a run. The corduroy lines were every bit as strong and thick as they had been that morning.

The onshore wind was almost breathless, untroubling to the feathering peaks that lined the beach. Sprinting, he flew into the house, tore himself out of his school clothes for the last time, unconcerned about flying buttons or broken zippers, pulled on a spring suit, and bolted out the door with a 6'o" under his arm. All before his mother could finish saying, 'is that you dear? How was your exam?'

His strength was still building as he ran hard down the stairs to the beach, across the sand and into the water. Wedging barrels rolled and thundered from a dozen peaks within the wide bay, calling him with wide open mouths. A total of eight guys out, everyone else obviously satiated by a long morning session in a lilting offshore, or sitting out the light onshore to await the late afternoon glass off.

It was shallow; there was no denying that. And it was pitching; no denying that, either. But get inside one of those spinning barrels and you had a chance to make it through the deepest eye you'd ever pierced.

If you were fast and strong.

And he felt fast and strong.

Paddling out to the peak was a breeze. Punching through the shorebreak, he felt more powerful and in control with every stroke, zeroing in on the zone until he was there, and he was ready. Ready to take it on, alone on the ocean, it seemed. He took a deep breath and tried to calm himself.

The power, the confidence and the sheer joy welling up within him was almost too much, a physical presence inside him, swelling and heaving, as restless as the blue ocean. He slowed his breathing, tried to understand the source of the feeling.

'I'm eighteen. I've just finished my physics exam, the final exam of my school career. I am officially free of the education department. Of tuck-shops and uniforms, and deputy principals with smarmy looks and incredibly efficient spies. I am not the smartest kid who ever walked the earth, but I will be successful because I have strength and determination, and I will work hard.

'And right now, at this time, I feel the full power of my youth and freedom. I am here, on my surfboard, free to take any wave I choose. This wave, right here and now, is mine.'

The wave had stood up as it approached the sandbank out of deep water, rearing and broadening like a cobra's head, ready to strike. He turned to paddle into it, his energy growing with the adrenaline rush, assurance and command coursing through his veins.

The bowl opened up beneath him as the wave picked him up lightly, like a grain of sand, and he was on his feet, dropping swiftly down the jacking face. Growing speed, steepening wall and pounding heart, he lent his strength to the wave and felt it grow in return. At just the right moment, precisely the right juncture, he stalled – threw his weight backwards on the board, planted his back foot, and jammed the tail into the meat of the wave, then pushed forward again to gather speed as he pulled into the barrel.

In an instant he was engulfed in the spinning, spitting eye, threading the deepening hole deeper than ever before. Noises ceased. Exams and school evaporated. The darkness within the pit seemed to grow denser, and time stood still. The barrel enveloped him, held him like an insect in amber.

That time was passing, he knew but didn't feel. How much time flowed beneath his board, around his potent form, through the spinning vortex, he couldn't tell. Nanoseconds? Years? It didn't matter. He was in the deepest, warmest passage of his life, deeply comfortable and profoundly at home. The barrel could go on forever, and he wouldn't know it.

He awoke startled. His eyes flashed open and confusion blew him away. The barrel? Where was it? Just a moment ago, he was in there, glorying. Now where was he?

Had he taken a head dip in the sand? Died of sheer pleasure in the tube? No, it was worse than that. In a rush, he knew. He was 34 years old and hadn't surfed in seven years. Just worked and worried. Pushed and found no place that yielded, tried and found no way out of the box he'd built around himself. Become the man he swore he'd never be, the day he'd ridden that barrel.

In the dark he rolled over, squinting at the clock radio. 4.45am. Sun up in three quarters of an hour. He sat up, started to pull on his trakky daks. His wife rolled over and in a sleepy voice asked, 'what are you doing?'

'Going surfing,' he replied.

When the horizon goes black

You know the feeling. It's pretty big, and you've already strayed to the wrong side of your comfort zone, but you're coping. You've managed so far by telling yourself the fear can be conquered. Repeatedly affirming that your only real enemies are hesitation and lack of confidence, and that pushing yourself over the edge of these moving mountains of water is an act of will.

The adrenalin surge you get with each successful ride is a powerful narcotic, and you want more of it. So you take the beatings and learn from them. Discover how to quell the rising panic when the hold down is longer and the thrashing more violent than you'd expected. You tell yourself the beltings are liberating. Empowering.

The rush of joy you get on breaching the surface after a brutal working by a venomous maelstrom is insane, and the elation you get paddling back out after a big, long ride is even more so. It's energising and addictive, so in spite of the underlying nerves you don't want to go in. You want to keep on pushing your personal envelope. And maybe your luck.

But then it happens.

That old saying about "the horizon going black" is, of course, a gross exaggeration. A piece, when you think of it, of ridiculous hyperbole so far from being realistic that it makes no sense at all. And yet, as it approaches, that wave fills your vision so completely, and its size and magnitude flood your mind so fully, that it seems as though the horizon has indeed gone black.

Taking off on the waves you've already ridden may have been an act of will, but this is a force of nature. This fear can't be conquered, because there's no way out of it. That fucking thing is going to mow you down. Grind you down and whip you and shake your bones, and rattle your brain and compress your lungs. Squeeze and flay you as it pushes you deeper and deeper into the darkness.

The terror mounts as the wave stands up in front of you, impossibly tall and monstrously thick, gaining size and momentum with every metre. You ask yourself how the fuck it came to this, and why you thought it was a good idea to be out there in the first place.

Then it throws over, top to bottom, and the thick, sledge-hammer lip slams into the flat water a few metres in front of you. Somehow it makes the whole ocean shudder. The noise is petrifying, and the wall of foaming horror is exploding towards you. In the last second or two – maybe *your* last second or two – you go through the pointless debate: should I or shouldn't I bail? Do I throw away my one and only flotation device and try to dive under the beast, or do I wrap my arms and legs around my board so that when the crushing vortex finally finishes with me, I'll go straight to the surface?

Either way, you know you're fucked.

The thing rolls over you like a white tank. A liquid steam train. It drags you down and tosses you up, rolls you over and twists you inside out. The fear is about to reach its apogee and the panic is about to overwhelm you when the storm abates. You're heading to the surface alive.

Breaking through into the air is the sweetest relief on earth. The taste of oxygen is beyond delicious, beyond supernatural. It's life itself. You made it.

You open your eyes and see the bigger one out the back feathering.

Soul Surfer

"Stoke that fire! I can't hear enough wailing! Excuse me, is that man smiling??"

Lucifer was doing his rounds, laying encouragement and tail whippings about him as he went. All the imps and fiends and junior tempters dashed about madly, trying to look busy as Old Nick toured their sections, and the souls clustered in each sector he passed through copped an extra dose of agony to impress the boss.

The Evil One swept dramatically into an Earth Monitoring Room and immediately the phalanx of apprentice devils working at their screens sprang to attention. Except one. Young Belial sat engrossed at a Monitoring Station, staring glumly at the image on his screen, unaware of the approach of the Beast. Fortunately, Beelzebub had a soft spot for young Belial – as much as any being that is consumed with loathing and bitterness can have a soft spot – and asked in his least hateful tone, "What's wrong, Bel?"

Hearing the voice of the Antichrist over the hellish din of the place – it really is pandemonium at times – Belial jumped to his cloven hooves and stammered, "Prince of Darkness. All sin is your glory…"

"Yes, yes, never mind that," hissed the Devil. "Just tell me what the bloody hell is wrong with you."

"Well," began Belial uncertainly, "great malefactor, I can't seem to get the gist of some human selling his soul to us. I mean, why should the human do it for a start, and what good does it do us?" The other devilkins gasped. This was heresy!

"I mean, why not just wait until they die and we'll more than likely get their souls anyway," continued the young demon, to the growing horror of his classmates. "Let's face it, they're just about all damned one way or another."

Fortunately, Satan appeared to be in a pretty relaxed mood, and indulged the young fellow, rocking back and forth on his long red tail as he listened, chuckling evilly every now and then. Then he looked at the assembled denizens of Hades and motioned for them to gather around.

"Listen up juniors, I'll explain this to you all at once, for Belial's benefit." The others looked at Belial with envy and hatred – *why would Satan be so nice to him?* – they grumbled. But obediently they crowded around the now beaming young imp's Earth Monitoring Station and turned their pointy ears to The Evil One.

"First, why would a human sell his soul to us? Easy. To get something he wants. Something that piety and goodness and prayer and all that other hokey bullshit just can't give him. Something truly satisfying in a deep, primeval sense. Something not connected with the intellect, or knowledge of what's 'right' and 'wrong'. A prize that transcends those stupid concepts and becomes 'spiritual', if you will. Just about any human will sell his soul to you in a few seconds flat if you offer them the right incentive. But why not just wait till they die, you say? Take a look at the screen." He jabbed the prickly arrowhead of his tail at the screen, where a typical Earth day was underway.

"These days there's a Jehovah, a Mormon, three Methodists and eleven Hare Krishnas on every corner down there. Souls are being saved like it's going out of fashion!" He bellowed so loudly that several of the less attentive apprentices jumped back a pace.

"We've got to get out there and collect those wayward souls before the bloody do-gooders get there first. Our mission is to wheedle, con and steal as many souls from as many people as possible, before they can be converted and lost forever."

Looking at the apprentices with a superior sneer, Lucifer was met with a collective blank stare.

"Okay. I can see that a demonstration is in order." With a playful tap that would have killed a horse, Mephistopheles swiped Belial from his seat, and took his position before the massive, multi-screened Earth Monitoring Station, his evil red hands resting lightly on the massive keyboard.

In a few seconds, he had a new image on the main screen. A photo of an ordinary, if scruffy and goofy looking young man.

"Damon Dowding. Twenty-four, a surfer. Works as a sign writer. Devoted to his girlfriend. Loves a beer and an occasional recreational substance, but is a genuine good bloke, and an all too likely candidate for a lifetime of niceness and a one way trip to the other place."

He swung around in the chair and stared with piercing malevolence at the apprentices. "Unless we do something about it, that young man is going to heaven!"

The apprentices all assumed a guise of horror and dismay.

"You may scoff, you young imps," spat the Dark Prince, even though not one of them had the temerity to even consider scoffing. That would have been particularly courageous, because if there's one thing that the great Seducer abhors, it's scoffing. At least, at him.

"But it's true – without our help, this bloke will never do anything bad enough to earn him a place in our little fire and brimstone gig. And we can't have that. So we need to get him to sell his soul. Any ideas how?"

A small, rather insignificant satyr put up his hand. "Errm, offer money?"

"Pah!" screamed the Devil. "Too obvious. So completely without finesse or art! No, we need to identify something that Mr Dowding here wants so badly, that he covets with such intensity, that he'll hand over his soul without even thinking about it. After that, the trick is to bring home the said soul as soon as possible, to avoid the possibility of late redemption and the irretrievable loss of it for all of eternity."

Again, all Satan could see was a sea of expressionless red faces flickering in the hellfirelight. Disappointed but undaunted, the Devil moved on.

"Jeez you're an unimaginative bunch aren't you? Look, let's have a deeper look at our subject here." At the push of a key with his grubby scarlet hand, the Polluter pulled up a live feed of the life in question. The assembled imps were watching a bedroom – small, nondescript and decorated with a number of surfing posters and strewn with dirty clothes. On the bed, Damon Dowding was masturbating over a video on a small electronic screen.

"Can't we get him for that?" asked an imp.

"Ha! If only!" Lucifer snorted. "If that were the case, we'd have 'em all!" And the rabble of apprentice archenemies laughed heartily at the Boss's little joke.

Damon finished his recreation and washed his hands in the bathroom before slouching off into the kitchen and began to fix himself a sandwich. The covey of demonettes watched all this with varying degrees of interest – for most of them the fun had stopped when the video had been switched off.

But then Damon took his sandwich into the living room and sat down in front of the television, and was immediately absorbed by whatever it was that he saw. The Serpent snapped to attention, followed swiftly by the gathered greenhorns. Damon was watching so intently that he forgot to even take a bite of his sandwich, and observing this the Soul Taker offered his cursed commentary.

"See the way this young simpleton's eyes glaze over and his jaw slackens. Obviously he lusts after whatever is on the screen. So all we have to do is offer it to him for the price of his soul, and he's ours. But a word of warning here – never let your target know that you genuinely want their soul, because you just won't get it. Subtlety is the key, and if you can achieve your aim slyly, with a dash of lying and cheating, so much the better. Now, just what is he looking at?"

With a deft touch on the keyboard, the Prince of Darkness changed the image on Belial's screen to show what Damon was watching: an unbelievably tall, thick, moving mountain of blue-green water exploding onto a reef in a torrent of power and beauty, while a maniac who showed up only as a dot on the face of the wave rode the beast, all confidence and adrenalin.

Outer reef Hawaii, maxing at forty feet. "Oh, this is too easy," gurgled the Vile One. "Too easy indeed. Watch and learn – this is a textbook case, and I reckon I can wrap it up and have that man's soul in here by the end of next month…"

It was the purple moment before dawn, and Damon Dowding was asleep next to his girlfriend Trudy. There was a faint rustle of the curtain by the closed window, and Damon woke up with a singular thought burning in his mind: "Surf's up!"

It was almost as though the thought had been planted in his head by an unknown force, and he was obliged to act on it. He jumped out of bed and got his gear into the car as quickly and quietly as he could, leaving Trudy blissfully asleep. Twenty minutes later he was at his local break, struggling into his wet-suit in the growing light.

Out on Styx Reef, perfect five foot peelers were barrelling along the coral with a muffled whump-thump, and there was just one other bloke out. Filth. Damon didn't recognise the bloke – he wasn't a local. In fact, oddly, the bloke must have had no car or bike or anything: Damon's was the only vehicle in the carpark. He shrugged and entered the water, paddling out into the lineup just as the sun rose over the hill to strike brilliant light onto the peak of the next set wave. The unknown surfer paddled into a six footer and immediately pulled in to a hell pit, his blood red board booming across the face like a rocket. He was still in the tube when he flew past Damon, howling like a wolf. "Whoever he is, he can bloody-well surf!" thought Damon.

For the next twenty minutes, it was as though Damon was alone with the waves – the only time he saw the other bloke was when he was on a wave and the other was paddling back out, and vice versa. It was one of the best sessions Damon had ever had at his home break – sensational waves that simply begged for big bottom turns and rewarded them with gaping barrels, followed by easy sections that allowed him to pound the lip like a madman.

And if Damon was ripping, the other guy was totally out of this world. You'd swear he was easily Top 5, but he looked like no one Damon had ever seen. Damon smiled broadly as he paddled out onto the peak and found the other sitting calmly on his red board.

"Fuckin' hellish day, eh mate?" he said happily. The other, in a tight, jet black wetsuit, with black hair and a Van Dyke beard and mo, grinned back.

"Hell yeah!" the bloke said. "And it's going to get better!"

As he spoke he paddled for a wave, and as he took off an echo of raucous laughter catapulted over the back of the rising six footer. The next time they met in the lineup (unbelievably, there were still just the two of them out), there was a bit of a lull, and they got to talking. The black-haired, bearded bloke seemed to have surfed just about everywhere, and knew just about everyone and everything.

"You ever surf Sunset?" he asked Damon, who shook his head.

"Never even been to Bali mate!" he laughed.

"My man, you should see Sunset at fifteen feet," enthused the other. "You don't wanna go, you don't wanna go, but the other guys are hooting and calling you into it, so you just go, and you just drive down, down, down the face for – whew – hours man, and – aaaaaaaaggghhh – you just arc into the heaviest bottom turn of your whole life, and it bowls up and – pyushhhh – you blow your load."

Damon shook his head and laughed. "Oh, that must be so awesome…"

"Oh it is," cooed the other with a gleam in his eye. "Most people I know would sell their souls for a trip to Hawaii. Would you?"

"Ha! Sell my soul for that? You've got to be kidding! I'm a greedy bastard. I'd want first class tickets, a brand new quiver and – and this is the most important bit – the balls to takeoff on a twenty footer. Still, it'll never happen, eh?" Damon was enjoying this silly conversation, one he'd had a hundred times before.

"Aww, I dunno," said the other bloke. "I reckon it could be done. Shake my hand and we'll call it a deal."

Damon stuck out his hand and the other shook it, laughing loud and hearty. Damon laughed along, but he also said to himself, "This guy's a nutter!"

Then, out of nowhere, there was a wave, and the other bloke turned and took it, still laughing like a drain. Damon never saw the bloke flick out of the wave, or get out of the water, but he didn't show up again on the peak – his laughter simply died under the sound of the wave, and he was gone. Almost instantly, the swell subsided to a fraction of its former size and the onshore breeze came in, and at the same time other surfers started paddling out, so Damon took the next wave in and went home. He didn't think about the other surfer at all, and in no time had forgotten the whole conversation.

Walking in the front door of his house a couple of days later, Damon was met by Trudy who, in a high state of excitement, threw her arms around his neck and wrapped her legs around his waist and squealed.

"You know how I entered that bikini model competition in that trashy surfing magazine, like, yesterday? Well I won!" she said with unrestrained delight. Thrilled for his girlfriend, and not entirely unmindful of the prestige this would carry with his mates, Damon planted a big kiss on Trudy's thick red lips.

"But that's not all," she continued in excitement bordering on delirium, "We get a pile of surfwear, a holiday in Hawaii, and a quiver of surfboards for you and a couple of boogie boards for me!"

Completely blown away by this incredible good fortune, Damon threw his head back and laughed and laughed and laughed. Deep in the bowels of hell, the knot of junior succubi clustered around the Prince of Darkness, and the Evil One himself, watched all this on Belial's Earth Monitor and joined Damon in his laughter.

Sauntering out of the airport in Hawaii, struggling with his new quiver (7'6", 8'4" and 9'11" guns), his beautiful blonde girlfriend beside him, Damon fancied he looked pretty cool.

In fact, he looked just like any of the brainlessly buoyant dickheads who lob on the North Shore each year in their eager thousands, dreaming of forging an instant reputation for taking on Hawaii's big waves and smashing them.

They checked into a swank hotel and celebrated with a massive dinner at a suave restaurant, drinking far too much and having a wonderful time.

That night, as they partied, the swell magically came up. And kept growing. By dawn the whole North Shore was echoing with the massive boom and crackle of big wave explosions.

Nastily hungover, Damon sat in front of the TV and watched the surf report. Endless sets of impossibly huge waves were throwing hundreds of tonnes of water onto the reef at Waimea. There were even sets that closed out the whole bay.

"I'm going out at Waimea," he said.

"Don't be ridiculous!" snorted Trudy. "Look at the size of those things. You'll be killed!"

"Nah, I'll be right", said Damon airily, taking his 9'11" out of its board bag. Trudy's eyes widened in horror as she realised he was serious.

"It's twenty-five feet at twenty-three seconds Damon," she whispered in terror. "You've never surfed anywhere bigger than Triggs!!"

"Hey," laughed Damon, "I've surfed big Triggs!"

Then, seeing the concern on Trudy's face, he added, "Look honey, don't worry. I feel so right about this. It's as though I've been. . .given the confidence and gifted the surf. Your charm and beauty got us here and won me these boards, and all I have to do is go out there and fulfill my destiny."

This did nothing to appease the fear growing in Trudy's heart, but she could see that he wasn't to be deflected. She watched in silent fear as he waxed up the long board, and left the room carrying a backpack with a towel, some wax and some sunscreen, to find a hotel driver. The drive up to the North Shore was one of tingling anticipation, burgeoning expectation at the heights to which his performance would soar, and glowing satisfaction that this was going to be the best day of his life.

His lack of fear was remarkable and encouraging. He felt like he owned the world.

The paddle out was diabolical. A shorebreak bigger than the biggest waves he'd ever surfed back home pounded the beach, and it took quite some time for Damon to punch his way through it and fight his way out to the lineup.

There were only a couple of dozen surfers on the heaving Waimea peak – most of them well known big wave riders. They eyed Damon with curiosity and not a little concern. One of them asked, "Are you sure you should be out here Brah?"

Damon figured that this was just localism, and he brashly said, "Be cool bro', I won't drop in on ya." The crew just shook their heads – they'd seen clueless accidents like Damon waiting to happen before – and watched an incoming set roll in off the horizon.

A mammoth swell, pushing the limits of what's rideable at the Bay, surged in and jacked up. Incredibly, Damon was sitting right where the wave peaked, and he had almost no option but to go. He paddled like a demon to get onto it, and suddenly he was up and hurtling down the skyscraper-sized face, adrenalin levels going through the roof, and his mind boggling at what he'd taken on.

His board was absolutely screaming and picking up speed. Down the face he plunged, faster, further, faster still and still dropping, accelerating madly, flying further and faster than he ever had before.

But not far enough or fast enough.

The diabolically thick, merciless lip threw itself off the top of the wave and came crashing down on him like a hundred tonne guillotine. The impact drove him straight through his board, smashing the wind out of him, and slammed him into the boulders deep below with immense and final force. With no breath, the crushing weight of the water and the fear of death all piling up on him, Damon had no chance of survival.

About twenty minutes later, the Waimea lifeguard dragged Damon's lifeless body from the shorebreak, still attached to a small remnant of the brand new board.

In the pit of eternal perdition, Old Nick turned from the Earth Monitor screen to grin at his gallery of wretches. "Too easy kids. Not only did I trick the poor bastard into selling his soul, I arranged a rapid delivery of same. Can anyone tell me how?"

Belial put up his thick red paw. "Umm, is it because he asked for courage, but not skill?"

The Devil grinned broadly and clapped Belial on the back. "Precisely my boy. Vain fools that they are, humans will always ask for what they want, but never what they need. And that makes our job so much easier. In this case, devilishly easy!"

He laughed and swept from the room, leaving the varlets to marvel at his prowess. As he moseyed down the flaming halls of his domain, the apprentices heard the echoes: "Stoke that fire. This oil is tepid! More brimstone here…NOW!"

The Last Wave

What would you do if you knew your next wave would be your last? The last wave of over thirty years of surfing. The last wave of your life.

James watched that last wave silently stealing towards him. It was coming on to dusk, and with a twenty minute boat ride from Karoniki Island back to Pulau Nyang-Nyang, they had to leave soon. Nura, the boat driver, wouldn't want to risk navigating the narrow channel to the beach in the dark. The others were already on the boat – his brother Luke, his mate Ferri, and their surf guide and host Glen.

Glen had agreed to allow this little group of three to come and stay at his Mentawai Islands resort two weeks before the regular season started because of James. As frequent guests on the island, James and his companions had become more like friends than customers, and Glen was open to the idea of one quick last trip before James went in for several more bouts of chemo- and radiotherapy.

James already knew it was futile. Felt it in his aching, weary bones. He'd been on the treatment merry-go-round for over a year, but the disease had paid no regard to that, and continued to spread. As fast as any radioactive or chemical assault on his body might kill cells and carry off his quality of life with them, the disease was too established. Too comfortable eating away at his body to be eradicated, or even significantly slowed.

But he wouldn't have missed this trip for anything in the world, pain or no pain. In fact, for long periods, the waves, the laughter, and the sheer tropical intoxication of it all had kept the stinging, gnawing, throbbing, stabbing misery at bay.

They'd had a blast. E-Bay had turned on for one afternoon – not epic, not wide open, but solid and fast enough for them all to get a few memorable rides. They'd scored a whole morning of fun-sized, creamy Beng-Bengs to themselves. Nipussi, six foot in the lightest of cooling onshores, had been surprisingly obliging. And a frustrating but hilarious early run to Pistols had yielded mateship and good-humoured roastings while waiting for the inconsistent sets.

At night, beers had been consumed and stories had been told while the jungle hummed, and away across the glistering water lightning storms flashed and flared over Siberut – close enough to see, but too far away to hear.

Such a tight-knit group. Such hot, wet nights. Such a lot of heavy silence and expectation enveloping the scene like a damp, warm blanket.

Tonight was to be their last night. In the morning the boat would speed them back to Sumatra, and James would go home to slowly die.

The air had a thick, soft purple feel to it. Not a breath of wind disturbed the silken blue water, and in the dense jungle of Karoniki Island, the darkness gathered.

Most of us, considering what we might do with our last wave, would brashly envisage ourselves shredding; ripping, gouging, tearing. Maybe looking for one last barrel, hoping to peek through the eye of hypnotic joy one last time, to hold that memory in one's mind until the black infinity descends.

James watched the liquid lump rising as it crept upon him, a seductive swelling of mirror-like perfection, and he didn't think any of those things. He felt calm. Thankful. At peace. He stroked into it easily as, fifty metres away on the boat, his mates hooted and whistled.

Burgerworld is an underrated and unfairly named wave. On its day it presents a fast wall, a couple of punchy sections ripe for a gouge, and a long, looping ride along the island's picture-postcard, palm-encrusted shore.

James's final wave was a typically friendly, forgiving, cruisy Burger's gem. Pulsing with enough power and speed to make it more than worthwhile, and served up with a beguiling mixture of exotic beauty and blissful atmosphere. His turns were solid and satisfying without being showy. Arcing white foamy water at the psychedelic sky, his style was graceful, unhurried. A thing of joy to be savoured slowly. Lingeringly.

It was the last wave of his life, the one he would remember as long as he lived, and James rode it to the end. The velvet sweetness of the water, the delicious scent-laden air, with colours in the sky changing every second, the dim echo of his crazy, caring, unforgettable crew cheering like madmen, the soft splash of spray as he carved his legacy into the welcoming wall – it would all stay with him and sustain him in the hard days to come. Maybe it wasn't everyone's idea of the perfect last wave, but it was his.

He paddled over, climbed up into the boat, and gratefully accepted an ice-cold Bintang.

The Point
(A true story)

Friday Night

Storms have been pounding the coast all week, with more expected next week. It's your typical winter scenario – loads of swell, conditions completely buggered. Our beaches have been copping a pounding and look like washing machines. But there is a window. Sunday, Monday, and maybe even Tuesday, the breeze will be right and there's bound to be swell at a Point we know. It's a three hour drive to my mate's shack in the forest, and the current plan is to drive down there tomorrow arvo. Then on Sunday morning take the white-knuckle pre-dawn run to the Point – forty minutes on livestock-infested roads, followed by an hour on a torturous four wheel drive track, also knee-deep in casual kangaroos.

Solid swell, a good mate, and a secret spot. Looks like a hell of a weekend coming up, and I'm well into my fourth can of liquid preparation. Excuse me while I get another.

Sunday morning 10am – the Point

Last night was bitterly cold and insanely clear. Troy and I spent the early part of the evening looking over his block and drinking beer, watching the colours change in the sky and the roos bounce up and down the valley. Then we moved inside and tried to keep warm, drinking red wine and solving the world's problems. It was an interesting, though in the end increasingly slurred conversation.

At dawn this morning we bolted down a can of baked beans and a coffee, settled Troy's dogs into the vehicle, and after two solid hours of dodging roos by the hundred and tackling the evils of the four wheel drive track, here we are!

This is a massive point about a kilometre or so across at its thickest, sticking out into the ocean on a coastline otherwise made up of tall, raggedly rocky cliffs. We're completely alone. Initially we went across to the right-hander – a classic point break that looks along mile after mile of cliffs, with hundreds of unknown, unridden tubing beachbreaks stretching away as far as the eye can see.

It's pretty big, and the swell is a bit southerly for the right, breaking wide fairly often, and although it's hard to tell from a couple of hundred feet up a cliff, it looks well over head high. So rather than take that on in its present gnarly state, we came across to the left-hander. As I write, solid ten foot walls are breaking right across the bay, totally maxing out the beachies. Way out to sea, the left hand point break is booming with fucking monsters I can't guess the size of, but they look big and they're a bloody long way away.

Troy has just gone off to meditate, leaving me here to throw the tennis balls for the dogs and scratch out my story. We'll sit around for an hour, see if the swell settles, and then take another look at the right-hander. Fuck it's cold!

Sunday night 7pm – Troy's place

What a sensational afternoon we had! Before heading back across the point, we walked, scrambled and climbed about 400 metres out along the left-hander side, to see if we could find a safe jump off point. An immense crust of black lava in great hexagonal boulders – fairly geometrical but broken, cracked, crumbling and worn shapes that make them a bastard to walk across – juts out into the ocean with weird ledges and inlets and beetles of rock that suck and blow, and even the most likely jump off spots look hideously dangerous.

As we climbed across the hard black rock we saw something in the distance, and when we got closer discovered that it was a garden gnome, set up facing the ocean, to just sit and watch the waves go by. Unbelievable that anyone would bother lugging the little shit across all those rocks, then leave him here. People find the oddest ways of entertaining themselves. Getting into the spirit of it all, we named him the killer gnome, protector of One Gnome Point.

By the time we got to the far end of the point we could see just how big the left-hander really was – and it was fucking enormous; triple overhead at least, and sucking evilly on the reef. Sort of pleased to find no safe jump-off point, we drove back across the point to the right.

From above, the right looked to have cleaned up somewhat, although the entire bay was alive with snaking corduroy lines and the air was thick with salt spray.

We grabbed our gear and followed the dogs down the steep track to the bottom. A couple of others turned up to watch as we were suiting up, but they obviously wanted to see how we would handle it. From the black stony beach, the waves looked fairly big, but also well shaped by the rocky bottom. I was ready first, so I gingerly stepped out onto a finger of volcanic rocks covered with barnacles and got ready to jump.

The sets started to look fairly intimidating down at water level, and as I waited, three huge mother sets in a row bombed the point. I was shitting myself. But suddenly it all looked calm, so I jumped. A little wave, no more than chest high, popped up out of nowhere, and I attempted to duck dive under it. That shitty little wave grabbed, rolled and slammed me onto a big, flat rock, pinned on my back with the board over the top of me, pushing me down.

When I came up I was standing in waist deep water, so I leaped back on the board and paddled like a bastard for the channel. By now the waves were looking fucking huge, and a full sense of the amount of water being shunted about assaulted me. I paddled over a couple of eight footers as Troy crouched on the rocks awaiting a break, intensely aware of how small, insignificant and deeply alone I was on the ocean. Nothing but miles and miles of deserted coastline endlessly taking a bashing from a heavy southern swell, and I'd arrogantly presumed to make myself a part of it.

My first wave was big, but way fat – I'd found a lucky wide one on the rip that runs out through the channel, not on the lava rocks by the point.

Troy got the break he was waiting for and paddled out, and as he approached me, a mountain of water broke about fifty metres further out and rolled towards us. Three of the motherfuckers later, we were miles from the right-hander point, sitting in a fast flowing rip.

We paddled, bobbed and flailed around for a while as the size and frequency of the outside sets continued to increase. While we were trying to figure out how to survive all this, Troy mentioned that when he'd made the jump, he'd been slammed onto the rocks too, and as soon as he got a second he checked his board for damage. He couldn't find anything, but he was suss.

It was pretty nervy out there amongst those heaving walls of water, with swirling rips and currents running through and around and over everything, but we managed to takeoff on a few, and started to get a feel for it. It was a bit too big for the point really, and most of the bigger ones closed out, but some had perfect shape, and we both stroked into a number of hefty drops, revelling in the monstrous grunt of those beasts as they thundered onto the lava below.

After we'd been out there about an hour and a half, a clean-up set came through and drilled us, but behind it was a perfectly directed and shaped trio of waves, ten foot I'd say. Troy took the first.

I took the second and dropped like a freight train into an impossibly long, steep wall that was about to shut down in a solid fifty metre section. As it closed out, I exited over the back, anxiously looking to see if there was another bigger one behind to deal me a bit of pain.

There were no more, so as I paddled out I looked for my mate. Over in the impact zone, treading water, Troy held up the back three foot of his seven footer.

Later, when he told me about it, he explained that he was a bit unhappy, because he'd taken a screamer of a drop, set up for a gouging bottom turn – and halfway through it the board had folded like a deck chair and left him doing nought miles an hour in front of a merciless lump of tumbling, frothing brutality. He reckoned he might have creased the board when he jumped off the rocks, and a fast, heavy bottom turn deep in the trough of that beast had done the rest.

Taking a head high wave into the beach, I left Troy to hang around in the lineup playing kickboard in big, dredging surf. I found the front four foot of his board up on a shelf, as he dragged his sorry arse over the crusty rocks to the safety of the beach. We packed up, climbed the bastard hill and had a beer overlooking the point before heading off. And because we'd taken on big, lonely surf, we felt like men.

It's almost 8.00pm now, and although it's still mighty cold, we're satisfied. Looking forward to a bowl of pasta, a bush shower and then rolling out the swag. Hoping for a swell drop tomorrow so the Point handles it better.

Monday night 6pm

A classic day at the Point. Tons of waves, heaps of poundings, a few cool people, and waves to fucking die for. Sleeping in till 7.00 this morning, we went into town first for fuel.

It was a gorgeous morning for a drive, and the lack of suicidal marsupials, wandering sheep and assorted other wildlife at that time of day made the track seem a bit easier than yesterday.

By 10.00am we were standing on the cliff-top looking at an ocean of clean swell lines buffed by a reasonably stiff offshore, and half a dozen surfers in the water eating up solid four foot right-handers off the eastern side.

A quick warm-up climb down the cliff, a bitchin' struggle to get into cold wet wetties, and we were away. Much easier to get out than yesterday, and on the break, incredibly good waves – a long, wall-y and sometimes playful ride if you got the right one, and an evil working if you muffed the drop.

It was kind of treacherous because at the last second the wave wraps heavily towards the point, and if you don't takeoff just right you're history. In the two or three hours we were out there, the crowd dropped off to nothing, and Troy and I surfed it alone again.

Because it was handling the size much better, we had a brilliant surf, most of it witnessed only by the dogs, Pepsi and Myer, who'd broken free of their ropes the minute we got in the water, and spent the whole time barking encouragement from the rocks.

After a couple of hours, I took what I reckon is the one of the best right-handers I'll ever get – a wall that curved away from me but held up, so that I screamed across it, pig-dog style, and once or twice even copped a cover-up.

It was an insane wave, and I figured I wouldn't do much better, so it was time for one more to shore. As I paddled out, a motherfucker set came through, and I paddled like shit to get through it.

By the time it was past, I was well out the back and in a rip. As Troy sat on the rocks getting warm and dry, I paddled on the spot for about twenty minutes before finally busting out of the rip and getting back to the peak. I was totally exhausted by the time I got in, but so rapt by the waves we'd had, it didn't matter.

We even made it back to the shack in time to chop some firewood for tonight. And the verdict on the day? Classic. Perfect. A lifelong memory.

And there's only one more surf to go before we fall back into the pit of corruption that is 'civilisation'.

Tuesday 2pm

Got out to the Point at dawn this morning, all the way discussing whether the swell would have jumped again with an impending front. But to our amazement, almost nothing was happening there – a tiny, almost knee-high wave smacked onto the rocks at the right, while a near gale-force offshore whipped foam flecks off the minuscule swell. A look at the left-hander revealed a similar, eerie flatness, so we took the long drive home. Filthy, smelly and incredibly knackered now, but by Christ it was a great few days. Pity I can't ever tell you where the Point is, because the killer gnome would come and get me, and then he'd come after you!

Bad Magic

Slouching into an uncomfortable aluminium chair, Calem Wright clutched an overpriced Bintang and stared at the people hustling around him. Sunburned bodies and cornrowed hair, smiles all round and big packages containing paintings, carvings and bags of good, honest Bali junk. Everyone was going home happy, tired and over-indulged. Except Calem.

The last couple of days had been miserable, fraught with stress and haunted by the danger that stalked him. He was desperate to get off the island and back home.

Taking a large swallow from the Bintang, he again tried to make sense of it all. Tried to understand what had happened to him. He couldn't believe the most straight up explanation, but he couldn't come up with any other. It must have been the magic. Bad magic.

Three days ago, six days into his first ever Bali trip and with three weeks stretching out before him, he'd been having the time of his life. His mate, Indo veteran Ryan, had carped at him for years to save the bucks to do a Bali run, and finally he'd caved. And wondered why he'd waited so long. The surf was everything he'd hoped it would be and more, and the people as beautiful and friendly as he'd heard, only sweeter and more laid back. Everything was so relaxed, so freewheeling and so bloody cheap it wasn't funny. It was like he'd just been born into a new and much more magical world than the one he'd left several thousand kilometres behind.

Ryan had taught him how to order two beers (*dua Bintang silahkan,* pronounced *sil-uck-un*) and how to say thank you ("It's *terima kasih,* but just say tearin' my carseat," Rhino had helpfully suggested), and showed him the sights from Kuta to Seminyak and beyond, to Tanah Lot and Canggu.

But most importantly, Rhino had introduced him to the Bukit. The legendary surf playground covering Balangan, Dreamland, Bingin, Impossibles, Padang-Padang and the mighty Uluwatu, and then around the corner to Nyang-Nyang, Green Ball and more.

In the first five days they'd surfed them all bar Padang-Padang, in conditions ranging from perfect to clinically insane. They'd scored pitching barrels, long, winding walls, dredging wedges and heaving drops.

Calem couldn't believe just how sublime it was both in and out of the comfortably warm water; the cheap, tasty beer; the friendly faces of the Balinese everywhere enquiring after his health and noting his apparent need for a massage, driver, singlet, bow and arrow, watch, sunglasses, plaited hair or painted nails; and of course the mind-boggling, utterly addictive waves.

On the sixth day, the ocean had really come to life. Eight foot lines marched in with steely precision across sheet glass water and unloaded on reefs and beaches all along the Balinese coastline, and Ryan and Cal had been transported straight to heaven. Or at least to its earthly outpost, the Bukit.

As dawn had split the sky with its usual sub-equatorial suddenness, they'd been walking out to the point at Balangan. Stopping on the last patch of soft cunje under the overhang of the headland, they waited until a lull in the pounding swell opened a window before plunging into the warm, dark blue sea and paddled like crazy to get across the impact zone before the next set.

For the first half hour, the smooth, ruler-edged lines of swell pouring into the bay had had a distinctly southern cast, so they'd wrapped perfectly around the jagged headland and zipped along the reef in mindless, mechanical precision – at Mach speed.

Even the ones the boys didn't make were exhilarating, offering a screamingly quick take-off, a lightning dance across a steepening wall, and a dash for the hole before the thing closed out. The ones they did make were beyond description, beyond even feeling – they were simply the rush of a lifetime.

To literally fly along those long, peeling walls, now being covered up, now pumping like bejesus to gather speed to make it across the next closeout section, was to live a lifelong dream.

But as the tide of surfers paddling out to join them had turned from a trickle to a torrent, the real, lunar tide had pushed across the reef so that almost every set became less makeable than the last, and they were left with the option of competing for suicidal closeouts or heading in.

They paddled in and sat in a *warung* for almost an hour, eating toasties, drinking juice and watching people and boards getting mashed in the growing surf.

"Mate, we're gonna have to do it," frothed Ryan. "We're gonna have to take on the crowd at Padang-Padang, show 'em what we can do. Coupla goofies like us dropping into triple-overhead barrels, covering ourselves in glory and hard-bodied women – what's not to love?"

He was right, of course. One of Cal's goals in coming to Bali had been to prove himself at the famously chunky left-hander, and here was his chance. He felt fit, the previous days had convinced him that he was surfing like a god, and he was ready. The confidence with which he'd threaded the speedy pits at Balangan that morning told him he could do almost anything at Padang-Padang.

"Skull that smoothie mate, next stop the green room at Padang-Padang," he'd shouted at Rhino.

Less than thirty minutes later they were standing on the grey concrete bridge overlooking the PP circus. The beach was alive with colour – bikinis, boardies, towels, umbrellas, hawkers, walkers, gawkers, big wave talkers, photographers and show-offs, and so many big boards Calem lost count.

Wiley Balinese sellers wandered this way and that across the small stretch of beach, tempting sunbathers with their wares. But the real action was out in the water. Flawless barrels, six foot and bigger, followed one after another across the reef, spitting and throwing like great green demons being chased and occasionally ridden by innumerable little black dots, the surfers.

Although from their vantage point on the bridge they couldn't properly see the peak or the main barrel section, just seeing the crowd, the swirling white water in the channel and the boiling peak at the head of Impossibles reef was enough to tell them it was smoking.

They were off their bikes, down the stairs, through that damnably narrow crevice in the rocks and onto the beach as fast as their legs could carry them.

Cal felt as if his entire surfing career had been leading to this moment. He thought of his performances over the last few days. Fun, crouching Bingin pits. Wide open faces that ran neatly from Temples most of the way to the Main Peak at Uluwatu on the high tide, begging to be shredded – and he'd gratefully complied. Punting high and freely in the Dreamland beachies as the drumbeat of 'progress' – the building of a new resort – had thundered on. And that morning's solid hollowness at Balangan. This was going to be a piece of cake – with extra icing.

Although the small peak was fairly crowded, the vibe in the water was unbelievably mellow. As usual there was a crew of ridiculously talented locals out there, not just scoring the biggest sets and deepest barrels, but keeping the air out there clear and warm and friendly.

Cal and Ryan slotted in easily. They were strong boys, good surfers in great shape, and they were eating this up. Sure it took a while to learn to read the waves, to pick the sections and make them work, but from the get-go they were stoked.

Paddling back out after a screamer, Calem watched from the channel, beaming as his mate dropped into a shrieking steamroller and disappeared over the ledge. The hoots from the cliff top told him Rhino had gone deep and come out clean, and he ached to do the same thing again himself.

He'd almost made it all the way out the back again when he spied a thick, glossy lump racing towards the pack. It looked a little wider than the last one, so he sprint-paddled out and to the right, slightly ahead of the mob paddling across from the inside.

At the last possible moment he stopped and turned to paddle into the silently swelling beast. A split second before the peak grabbed him, he caught a flash of movement on the very edge of his periphery, and heard a soft but clear whistle. Someone was inside!

"Fuck him, I'm going," he thought as he pushed one more handful of water behind him and felt the surge. The green wall stood up sharply under him and he gripped the rails of his board, giving away his last chance to pull back.

As he stood, he heard a faint "*Ya!*" against the deep bass boom of the wave exploding, and ignored it. This wave was just too good not to take. Dropping almost vertically down the glistening mountain, he knew he was going to cut straight across the other surfer's path, but it was far too late to change course. Calem was committed to his line and the other bloke would have no choice but to fade into the white water. To straighten out right in front of the cliff and accept a brutal beating, probably laced with a fair amount of coral contact.

He turned his eyes to the wall in front and lost himself in the art and science of making the tube. He fixed his vision on a point just ahead of where he wanted to be, allowed the silver curtain of water falling to his right to enclose him, pumping his board in short, rapid beats to outrun the thickening wall on his left. In just a few tingling, tangled seconds he was being shoved out onto the mid-section, where he threw a sharp bottom-turn-to-stall, to set up for the inside barrel. He was listening for the hoots from the hill as he ducked into the second, smaller and tighter barrel, but they didn't come. He didn't care, of course. This was the day, this was the wave he'd been waiting for his whole life. And he knew he needed more. He paddled back to the lineup quickly, feeling golden, and scanned the horizon for his next victim.

As he sat quietly flexing his pecs and feeling like superman on a 6'6", a Balinese surfer paddled over to him. Flecks of blood on the bloke's shoulder told him this was the man he'd dropped in on, but he was smiling gently.

"Hey *Teman* (friend)," said the Balo. "Nice waves today, *ya?*"

"*Ya*," said Calem. "*Bagus* ay."

"You should, you know, maybe open your eyes and ears when you surf out here, *Teman*," said the Balinese. "We say '*hati-hati*'. It mean be careful. Because the magic here, it can turn dark, you know. If another *orang* is on the wave, *jangan* drop in, very dangerous."

"Yeah, whatever," said Calem carelessly. He wished this guy would leave him alone and go back to selling watches or whatever it was that he did.

"We have to share our beautiful Bali with many people," said the Balinese surfer. "But we have our rules too. Please do not drop in again, *Teman*". Calem turned a cool eye on the Balinese. There was no anger in the local's voice or eyes. He simply looked as if he was patiently explaining, yet again, to yet another newcomer, that even here in paradise the universal rules of surfing applied.

"Yeah, whatever," repeated Calem. "Go fuck yourself."

The Indonesian looked at him in surprise but said nothing. He lay down on his board and paddled away, muttering quietly to himself. As he paddled away, he kicked, and the splash showered Calem, who, far from being intimidated, felt infinitely superior to the islander.

At that moment, he felt strong enough to deal with anybody in the lineup who might take issue with his attitude, and he was focused on getting another one of those wonderfully throaty pits. So he didn't give the incident another thought, and turned his eyes and his thoughts to the horizon.

But the energy seemed to have changed somehow. For the rest of the session he was a man in the wrong spot at the wrong time. He'd paddle for one that looked good and the wave would fade out underneath him, or he'd go too deep and too late, and have to jump ship and end up getting annihilated by the roiling white water.

Ryan was still pulling into anything and everything and making them all, but for forty odd minutes Calem could get nothing. He finally managed to takeoff on a wave, not a set wave but a solid lump of Indian Ocean nonetheless, and felt the adrenalin kick in as the wall steepened. Pushing into a late, near-horizontal bottom turn, he caught the faintest edge of inside rail, bogged and was thrown off the front of the board.

At first, he just skimmed and bounced across the swiftly flowing water. But then the lip drove into him like a giant wedge and slammed him down into the waiting coral. In the dark seconds that followed, he rolled and rag-dolled across the reef, feeling clumps of flesh being torn from his shoulders, arms and back, waiting for the blow to his head he was sure would come.

At last he surfaced, gulping great gobfuls of air, only to see the first of a set of eight footers bearing down on the peak. He tried desperately to get to his board, but it was still tombstoning in the white water, and he wore the first wave of the set fair on the head. Three more flogged him, and when at least he got back on his board, he paddled limply back to shore, beaten. Look at the bright side, he told himself: his board was still in one piece, even if it did have a couple of new pressure dings on it.

The cuts and grazes weren't too bad either – they wouldn't keep him out of the water. But that didn't stop him screaming like a banshee later, when Rhino scrubbed them all and bathed them in Die Da Yao Jing. And although he was a little uncomfortable on the hard mattress in their room at the *losmen*, Cal slept well and woke up ready for a new day's surf.

At seven, he and Ryan jumped on their hired scooters and headed down the road to the Bukit. Given the still-solid swell hitting Kuta Beach, they figured they'd assault the Racetrack at Uluwatu on the low tide before maybe heading back to Padang-Padang.

Sitting at the traffic lights at the intersection at the end of the airport runway, waiting for the green, Calem looked at the statue of the gun toting 'hero' in front of him. He struggled to see how the smiling, peace-loving, friendly people of Bali could venerate a war man. But he guessed that it was the government of Indonesia that had decided to put it there; he couldn't imagine the Balinese having a dark side.

The light changed to green, and he moved to go. As he did so, a woman on a scooter stacked with children, crates and even a chicken cut across in front of him. He jammed on the front brake just as the front wheel entered a puddle left by the over-night rain, the wheel locked up and he went down on the road.

He huddled into a tight, frightened ball as the rest of the bikes, cars and buses swirled around and past him, oblivious to his plight. His fall had attracted the attention of the police-man permanently stationed at the intersection, and the cop came over, helped him push his bike to the side of the road and demanded to see his international licence. Cal showed him the document, and the cop scowled at it for a moment before pronouncing that Cal had caused a traffic disturbance and would be required to pay an immediate fine of 300,000 rupiah. That was his entire budget for the day – enough to cover a couple of smoothies and a jaffle or two at Uluwatu, and maybe a Bintang at the end of the day – but he paid up. He was sure the cop would be quite happy to drag him off to a cell somewhere if he was foolish enough to refuse.

Just down the road he found Ryan waiting for him. His mate had been unwilling to go back and maybe risk getting fined himself. They had a brief yak on the side of the road and agreed that it was probably not such a bad outcome, and there was no reason to stop now, so they kept on to Uluwatu. When they got there it was just what they'd hoped – pumping six foot, gaping barrels howling down the Racetrack reef, and less than two dozen surfers spread across the whole bay, most of whom appeared to be witless kooks.

The boys dragged their boards out of their board covers, and Calem found that his dinky little fall had knocked out two fins as well as the plugs holding them in. He sat in a *warung* on the limestone cliff face, watching Ryan score shack after booming shack and waiting while a local bloke who called himself Doggy repaired his board.

An hour and a half later, the board was fixed, Calem was another 400,000 rupiah lighter, and the tide had come in enough to wreck the barrels on the Racetrack. To top it off, the trade wind had clocked around a few degrees so that it was sideshore on the main peak, and getting more and more crumbly by the minute. Determined to surf, he paddled out to join the hungry, scrambling crew of about seventy maniacal blow-ins.

It was a dismal session that reminded him of shonky afternoons at home. Eventually he paddled in, disgusted. He found Rhino sitting happily in a warung, scoffing jaffles and juices, chatting to an assortment of attractive Nordic looking women barely wearing their bikinis. As soon as he sat down, the bevy found that they had an appointment elsewhere, and deserted the warung. His mate waved them a cheery goodbye. Rhino offered to buy him a jaffle, so they sat there and ate, watching the conditions and the swell deteriorate before heading back to Kuta.

The plan was to have a little *istirahat* (rest) in the losmen, then to go play on the lively sandbanks at Padma Street in Legian. Instead, Calem spent the whole afternoon alternately shitting and retching over the brown-encrusted toilet. Obviously something in his jaffle had gone down sideways and was trying to get back out any way it could.

Ryan, while full of sympathy for his mate, wasn't about to change his plans. He left Cal shivering in the losmen and walked down to the beach. An hour and a half later he came back glowing with satisfaction. "The rip was turning on a bit here and there but the banks are fuckin' perfect!" he bellowed. "It was just fuckin' awesome!"

Rhino sipped a Bintang while Calem struggled to keep down a mouthful of water, and they talked. "I dunno mate, this is all a bit fucked up," said Calem. "Yesterday I was having the time of my life, and suddenly it's all gone to shit and I'm having a really fucked up time, and I don't know why."

"Mate, I told you before we came, you gotta be careful. This is Bali and the stories about magic aren't all bullshit. There's dark magic here as well as light, and if you cross the line with any of the locals, or just do the wrong thing, you're pretty much fucked. So what happened?"

Calem told his mate about the incident at Padang-Padang and the other shook his head while he listened.

"And you told him to go fuck himself? Holy shit mate, no wonder the bad spirits are all over you. It was bad enough dropping in, but to then follow it up by being an arrogant white bastard, you're begging for a bit of karma. You should've apologised to that bloke."

"Yeah well I'm a decent bloke," wailed Calem. "How can I lift this curse, or hoodoo voodoo or whatever it is?"

"For a start, take it seriously mate," said Ryan. "Second, find the bloke and settle it."

The next morning's surf check revealed pristine lines of powerful swell stacked to the horizon and rolling in sweet, unbroken rhythm towards the island. They made haste to Padang-Padang, where they sat and watched. Serial sets of over eight foot were blasting the PP coral, and the lineup was a crazy mix of carnage, heroism and blindly optimistic idiocy. They both wanted terribly to go out there, but Calem knew at best it would be stupid, at worst it would be suicidal, so they sat and watched and waited.

At last they saw the Balinese guy that Cal had dropped in on emerge grinning from the water and walk up the beach. Cal walked down to meet him and stopped him on the sand. "Hey mate," he said.

The Balinese looked at him with curiosity, and offered a happy, "Hey T*eman, apa kabar?*"

"I'm the bloke who dropped in on you the other day," said Calem. "We had a few words in the lineup afterwards and I think I was a bit rude eh. And since then things have been going pretty bad for me, you know, so I wanted to say I'm sorry. I'll never do it again, and I swear I'll show respect. But can you please lift this curse or whatever it is?"

A soft laugh escaped the Balinese man's thick, round lips, and he showed his white teeth. "Ah, you have bad spirit magic. Too bad *Teman*," he said. Then he laughed softly again. "Ha ha ha ha ha ha ha."

"Mate, you've gotta help me," said Calem. "I've got another three weeks here and I can't live like this. I been sick, I been fined, I been outta the water, and when I get in I don't get any waves. So can't I just say sorry and we'll leave it at that?"

"No *Teman*, you cannot. You have bad spirit now, you are in the hands of the gods. You can say sorry to me but it means nothing. You must say sorry to the gods. And maybe give them an offering."

"Will things get better if I do?" asked Calem.

The Balinese shook his head and smiled. "No," he said. "If you make a sacrifice and wear the black and white checks you see on our statues to keep the evil spirits away, maybe things will not get worse. But better? No."

"So what can I do?"

"*Pulang.* Go home. When you come back, maybe the bad spirits will not recognise you any more, and if you bring respect for Bali people and Bali waves, maybe you will have good times. But for now, the spirits know you have no real heart for Bali, and they will do keep doing bad things," he shrugged.

That night, Calem burned his board on the Balangan headland, offering the smoke to the gods and pleading for their protection. He went straight back to his *losmen*, stopping only to buy a black and white checked sarong, which he kept about him the whole night. In the morning he called the airline and changed his ticket to the first available flight home. Over two weeks early.

The call for his flight came across the PA system, and Calem stood up, tightened the sarong around his shoulders, and walked into the departure lounge. He'll go back to Bali again, hopefully a much wiser man. But who knows what the gods – good or bad – will have in store for him then?

The Island

There were other people on the ferry, but Kingo didn't really notice them. The beat of *Rage Against the Machine* blasting from his earphones straight into the centre of his brain blew almost everything else out of comprehension. Only the feeble vibrations of the engine below and the gently rhythmic rise and fall of the boat on the swell penetrated his consciousness. It had been a while since he'd last taken the boat ride to the island. Too long.

So now he was excited. The oily smoothness of the water's surface and the insistent rolling of the swell made him tense with anticipation. He knew there'd be good surf, and he knew he'd be riding it well. Somehow, every cell in his body knew it, individually and collectively. Sitting somewhere behind him at the stern of the ferry, his 6'2" surfboard knew it too, he thought.

"Together we'll carve," he said to himself, smiling. The board, the waves, his music machine, his backpack carrying his wetsuit, wax and towel, and his bike were all he'd need that day. He was a surfer alone, and anything or anyone more would be an intrusion.

She crossed his mind like a cirrus cloud driven by a jet-stream sweeps across the sky, scudding swiftly across the face of the sun and causing only the briefest afterthought of a shadow. Enough to be noticed, to make you to look up questioningly, but not enough to leave any lasting impression. Or to draw away the warmth of his solitude. Not even she could disturb his sense of peace today.

"It's over," he thought simply, and it was. She was gone, and the next song – a hard and heavy head-banger – detonated like a punk explosion in his head, and he sat there rocking to it and digging life.

The interminable process of swinging the boat into the jetty, tying up and setting the gangplank in place only heightened his anticipation, and Kingo stood at the doorway tapping his foot with a surfeit of energy, waiting for the deckies to let him out. By the time he walked down the aluminium gangplank, his board was already on the jetty and he could see that his bike would be coming off in a second.

"Perfect," he thought, turning his gaze towards the main-land, hoping to feel the brush of a north easterly breeze against his cheek as he did so. He did.

"Fuckin' perfect!" he thought again, and turned around in time to see the deckie on the upper deck of the boat hand his trusty treadly down to another crewman on the ground.

He grabbed the bike, strapped the board into the rack mounted on its rear, adjusted his backpack, hit the play button on his music maker, and was off.

Out through the centre of the busy Thomson Bay Settlement, dodging hungover holiday makers weaving their way up to the bakery for a fresh loaf and a sugary donut; past the knobby hill on which Vlamingh's Lookout sits, and onto the causeway between the shallow salt lakes. He nodded good morning to the sandpipers pecking along the shoreline of Herschell Lake, and a clutch of feeding ducks showed him their feathery bums.

There were few people around, and he saw no surfers cycling in either direction – *oh please let there be no crowd!* he pleaded to no one in particular. Up the big hill past where a farm used to be, he concentrated on riding, and by the time he got to the top he was sweating. But the big hill was the only really major effort on the way there, so he didn't stress about it.

The long straight stretch – the one with the three green-cloaked hummocks that reared up one after the other, and which he and his mates called The Three Bitches – came and went fairly easily. Then he was coasting down the hill past the Quokka Stop, where the tourist buses disgorge passengers so they can experience the joys of hand-feeding a furry little rodent. As if there weren't enough quokkas in the Settlement who'd gladly accept the odd morsel. Or, indeed, who will hop straight into your kitchen and start scrounging if you're staying on Rottnest.

The road twisted around a bit for the next few hundred metres, then he was on the peak of the hill that offers the first glimpse of the ocean on the southern side of the island. From that vantage point he could see the broad expanse of Salmon Bay, from Salmon Point in the east, past Nancy Cove and Green Island all the way to the tip of Mary Cove, which sits next to the eastern end of Strickland Bay. One glance told him what he wanted to know: that the wind was near enough to directly offshore at Stricko's, and a reasonably healthy swell was steamrolling in from the south. Filth!

Conditions perfect, body tense with excitement, almost there. He flew down the hill, whipped around the bend at Green Island and powered up the short stretch of road before the Strickland Bay track turn-off. It's a boggy, sandy bitch of a thing, the Strickland track, and by the time he reached the toilet block built by the Offshore Boardriders Club, Kingo was both swearing and sweating with equal immoderation.

There were only four other bikes in the parking area, and he swore he could hear a faint booming from over the hill. But he took the time to carefully chain his bike to the wooden railing. His love of solitude didn't extend to the long, solitary walk back to the Settlement after having his bike stolen.

That had happened once, that his bike – a hire bike – had been pinched from this spot while he was surfing. When he'd discovered its absence, he'd simply shrugged and set off for Thomson Bay, seven and a half kilometres away. But the heat, the lack of shade and the legions of flies that infested his personal space had effectively wrecked any chance of enjoying the walk, and he was glad when a passing bus from The Lodge had picked him up about halfway back.

So on this day, in spite of his acute desire to dart over the hill and get amongst it, he carefully secured the bike before walking up the short path to the crest overlooking the break.

Kingo felt instantly blessed. Right in front of him, not 150 metres away, a swirling A-frame peak was standing up on the reef, a white plume streaking off it, and breaking, breaking, breaking in a slow, powerful performance of natural beauty.

One very lucky man was carving a white foam path across the right hand face of the wave. Another surfer was paddling back out to the lineup, and five more sat spread across the bommie - the 'bubble' on which the Stricko's wave begins to break.

He trundled happily down the hill and walked along the rocky-sandy beach to the spot where he habitually deposited his gear. He'd long ago chosen that spot for two reasons. First because it was directly in front of the break, allowing him to check out how it was breaking, the state of the reef and the whirlpool in the impact zone, while he changed into his wet-suit. And second because it allowed him to paddle out through the channel at the western side of the break rather than walk out on the reef on the eastern side and risk getting eaten by a set before getting through the impact zone. Today, with frequent sets in what looked like the six foot plus range, paddling out in the channel seemed the wiser approach.

He watched as he struggled into his wetsuit. The peak was tall and steep, and on the left – which he'd be riding most of the time – the first section jacked up and pitted heavily, making a successful shoulder take-off highly unlikely.

That meant a deep, fast takeoff on the peak, a hard, sharp bottom turn in the critical part of the bowl, and a race across the first section, with the possibility of a big, quick barrel. Make it out of that gaping hole, and there would be a slightly fatter workable section allowing a gouging cutback or an eye-popping re-entry, depending on the state of the lip and the size of the wave. Then, maybe, an opportunity to pull in for a longer freight train tube – taking care to get out of there and off the wave before the whole lot slammed onto the ledge.

Leave your exit too late and you're likely to end up with

bits of reef in your bum, back or head, and more than likely to get stuck in the whirlpool that sucks and seethes around the tabletop reef, making it one hell of a nasty impact zone. Even experienced surfers can get stuck in there, getting pounded on a heavy day – inexperienced punters often lose several minutes trying to extricate themselves from the hellish maelstrom.

Kingo had surfed Stricklands plenty of times, and he knew the wave, but no two days at Stricko's were ever alike, apart from those few constants like the tabletop reef and the whirlpool. But that's what made Stricklands such a challenge and a joy to Kingo – you just never knew what to expect or how to handle it until you were on the wave. In it. Under it, if you handled it wrong.

He took time to stretch – calves, thighs, groin, back, lats, stomach, pecs, shoulders, arms, neck. He was frothing to get out there, but he knew he'd need every millimetre of flexibility and reactive speed once he was there, so he went through the ritual slowly, pointedly.

And then he was walking across the reef, picking his way over the little weed filled chasms, and finally waiting just a couple of seconds for a foaming wash to surge over the edge of the reef so he could jump, board first, into the channel.

Paddling hard, he skirted the tabletop reef, then angled out towards the peak a hundred or so metres away. While he paddled, he watched the break, the reef, the sky; searching for clues as to what to expect when he got out the back, almost nauseous with excitement.

As he stroked on, feeling the strength in his arms, a set came through. A surfer on the peak caught the first one, and Kingo watched entranced as man and board plunged quickly down a near vertical face, chased by a thick, white, intense lip that crashed heavily on the dark water just behind him. The surfer obviously knew what he was doing – he kept going straight towards shore until he was a long way in front of the moving wall, then heaved into a deep, hacking bottom turn that drove his board back around to face the wave.

He turned inwards and crouched in one swift movement, and was engulfed by the spinning cylinder. A second later he shot out of the tube and set himself up for a carving cut-back. But Kingo didn't see the cut-back, because the wave was past him and he was paddling hard to get over a bigger wave that was marching solemnly towards him, with another behind it.

And then he was out on the peak, alone. Everyone else had caught a wave on that last set and was paddling back out, except for one who was paddling towards shore, his ragged movements showing that he was exhausted. He'd probably taken a sick beating at the hands of a set while Kingo was paddling through the channel, and then got himself stuck in the impact zone.

On the peak, right over the bubble, Kingo sat up on his board and looked around. As he was alone out there, he allowed himself a broad grin and spoke softly. "Mornin' Huey. Pleasure to be doin' business with you."

He surveyed the scene with satisfaction. The sky was an endless, depthless blue, the wind a mere capful and from precisely the right direction. Away on the south western flank of the island, a little further out to sea and therefore an indicator of things to come, the frothy signs of a potent swell terminating on deserted reefs drove his sense of anticipation up another notch. Seconds later, a dark mass of water reared up from the depths just offshore of him and steamed towards him. It was already feathering at its tall peak.

"Christ, it's big."

He paddled towards it as quickly as he could, and at the last moment turned and paddled into it, looking forward but seeing nothing until it picked him up and lifted him two, four, eight, twelve and more feet above where he'd just been. When he'd reached the very top, it shot him forward.

In the same instant, he was on his feet and his board was dropping beneath him, pointing almost straight down at the rocky and, he could see now, alarmingly shallow reef below. His body automatically went into full stretch and his arms shot straight up above his head as the board slid down the towering face gathering a hideous amount of speed.

He held his bottom turn until the last, critical moment, jamming so hard that his whole body was almost horizontal and his hands, now just in front of his chest, skimmed the water's surface. The board pivoted around to face along the wave, and he moved into a semi-crouch, leaning forward to gain maximum velocity. The wall of water obligingly steepened, turned into a pit, really, and the lip threw itself over him in a gleaming silver curtain. He was in the tube for just the briefest few seconds, but while he was in there time seemed to dilate. With every passing millisecond he felt bolder, stronger, more elated and more splendidly isolated.

He bolted out of the tube like a bullet from a gun barrel and stood up straight to guide the board along the gathering wall. Abruptly, he planted his weight on his back foot, to ram the board into a heavy cut-back. The sharp carving noise that rasped out from the fins under his feet was music to his ears, and his eyes delighted in the arcing white mane of water the rail threw up. But he didn't have time to admire his work – there was more to be done. He leaned hard left to bring the board around and dug his left hand into the wave to slow. As he did so he saw that the wave was starting to wedge up, the tabletop ledge looming fast. He flicked up and over the menacing lip, and the momentum he'd gathered and the force of the lip catapulted both him and his 6'2" high into the air. He hooted as he flew over the back of the wave, and splashed down in the clear water as the last of the wave spent itself on the ledge.

He paddled back out grinning fiercely, ecstatic with the wave, the tube, the day. As he reached the peak he noticed that two of the others were leaving the water, walking up the beach, and that made him feel even better. The smaller the crowd, the more he liked it.

So often the crowding at Stricklands annoyed him, occasionally even almost ruined his surf. And far too often, even in a small crowd, a familiar or vaguely recognisable face would appear at his elbow, its owner wanting to chatter incessantly between waves.

He wasn't into that. Even when he went surfing with his best mate, he kept pretty much silent in the lineup, preferring to be alone with his thoughts and his ocean. Sure, every now and then he'd offer a comment to someone he'd seen pull off a good manoeuvre, or say g'day to a mate. But he was never in the surf for 'company'. If he wanted to talk or meet people, he'd be in a bar somewhere, or hanging out with friends.

Out in the lineup, where the quality of his surf depended on having a clear and open mind and a calm spirit, distractions could be costly, and socialising with other surfers wasn't high on his list of priorities.

It wasn't that he was an anti-social being – he loved his family and friends as much as the next man, and on occasion really relied on having them around. And there was nothing he enjoyed more than sitting down with friends for a meal, a beer session, a long, obscure and entangled argument, or even a personally revealing conversation. But all in the right place at the right time.

Out on the water, with the sky at maximum depth, the nuances of the wind, the colours of the water and a hundred other things to concentrate on and enjoy, why waste time with idle bullshit? It was something that he never could understand. Or even tolerate really.

So the thinning crowd made him feel stronger in his solitude, more impenetrable in his fortress of self. It didn't bother him that some people might call him an egoist.

The only people who could really believe that such a feeling as contentment within oneself is selfishness, are those afraid of their own company. He felt that people who constantly seek out others often believe that they are gregarious when in fact they're simply unable to talk comfortably with the one person who is always there – themselves.

Such people are the truly lonely, yet they're the ones who would often look at Kingo, shake their heads and say, "it's so sad – he's always alone," in tragic tones. Not realising that just because it would be tragic for them to be alone with them-selves, it need not follow that everybody feels the same way.

He chuckled a little as he scanned the horizon for incoming swell. Somehow his thoughts on days like this always turned to the difference between loneliness and being alone. Maybe he was justifying to himself his conscious rejection of the company of others. But more likely he was recognising a truth not well known.

A dark lump of energy raced towards him, growing as the water became shallower beneath it, and he turned and paddled for the wave, his thoughts only on the business at hand.

Three hours later, Kingo was alone on the water, indeed, alone in the entire bay, waiting for one more wave to take him in. The sea breeze had shown up at long last, turning the smooth waters into a lumpy white-capped soup.

The waves were crumbling, closing out, harder to ride. But Kingo was cool with that. He'd had over an hour of solo surfing in spectacularly ideal conditions – the last of the crowd had long since headed back to the Settlement – and he'd surfed his guts out.

He thought about the people he knew and the people he liked and the people he'd have to deal with back at the Settlement, and he was ready to rejoin the human race, as it were.

A small, fat wave came through and he took it, holding on right until it thumped on the tabletop reef as he pulled a close-out re-entry over the shallow rock, diving off into the foam behind the wave before he hit the reef itself.

He picked his way across the reef to shore. When he reached the spot where his gear was stashed he grabbed the board bag and put the dripping wet 6'2" in it, being careful to not get even a single grain of sand on it. As he shoved it into the board bag, he said, "thanks man, that was a hell surf." Then, realising that he was talking to himself, said "Christ, I'd better get back to civilisation – I'm talking to a fucking surfboard now!"

He rode back to the Settlement slowly. His limbs were unwilling to expend the last of their rapidly diminishing energy reserves, the freshening sea breeze was a gruelling headwind in places, and he was relying on the sassy beat of a cruisy hip-hop number to keep his legs moving. By the time he rode into the Thomson Bay village he was aching for food and water, so he rode straight to the bakery and picked up a potato pie, a litre of mineral water and a fresh cream donut.

He sat in the shopping quadrangle, lazily watching holiday-makers mill about, jealously guarding his meal from the shameless gulls that will take any opportunity to steal food. He knew that they'd often come in from over his shoulder to take him by surprise, so he sat hunched over like an old man, and kept his pie low, near his stomach.

Once he'd eaten, he couldn't decide whether to take a nap or go to the pub for a beer and a bit of a read. He figured that if he was really in need of a nap, nothing would bring it on faster than a beer, but he was also wary that he might run into someone he knew at the pub, and he wasn't quite ready for full-on *bonhomie*.

Still, he struggled into his backpack and jumped on the bike to ride to the Quokka Arms. Once there he found a table with a bit of shade over it and set himself up with a beer and his book of the moment, Elias Canetti's *Crowds and Power*. Reading it, he began to grasp the insidious nature of crowds, and to more appreciate the attractions and benefits of solitude.

Mobs are susceptible to suggestion and easily moved to violence, anarchy and destruction. They consume the individuals that make them up, robbing them of any uniqueness or worth – in a crowd every participant is expendable and replaceable.

A man alone is an island, proud and unassailable.

In the hour and a half that he was there, Kingo was left happily alone, and only spoke when ordering middies. The barman knew Kingo as an island regular, but also knew of his penchant for being alone, so he didn't try to strike up a conversation, merely saying, "g'day" and, "no worries" at the right times.

At four o'clock Kingo stepped onto the ferry, found a seat on the top deck and continued reading. He remained blissfully undisturbed throughout the crossing, and when he got off the boat in Fremantle the throng was virtually invisible to him, so absorbed was he in his own world.

When he pulled up in his driveway at home he saw that his housemate was out and the house was empty, and for the first time that day he wished for someone to talk to.

All trip and no surf

I'm never going on a surf trip with Flathead again. The last one was classic Flathead, which means disaster from start to finish and weirdness through the middle. And, as usual, not a single wave ridden. Let me tell you about it.

He rings up in a state of high excitement (and yes, I do mean that literally, because he's yammering so quickly and confusedly I can tell he's been having weed for breakfast again) jabbering about a certain spot in the desert about 500k from here. Which he swears is going to be firing for the next few days, so we need to drag our flabby arses up there, like, instantly.

I should be suss about going anywhere with Flathead after all these years, but it sounds good to me and I can't resist the lure of a cylindrically flawless desert reef.

I call another mate, Lychee, and convince him to join us. I get my shit together and pack the car in under ten minutes, then swing by Lychee's place where he's already out the front with his gear. We're like a well-oiled machine.

We head around to Flathead's place, amped to get on the road and be there for a late arvo surf. After forty-five minutes of rooting around trying to find his sleeping bag, camp stove, wetsuit, fin key and other sundry crap, the Flatman is finally ready and strapped into his seat.

As we ease out of the driveway he says, "Oi, just gotta make a quick detour, ay". This so-called quick detour turns out to be to an inland suburb about thirty minutes in the opposite direction to where we're going. He directs me to stop in front of a dirty, broken down cesspit of a house complete with car wrecks, smashed windows and a jungle for a garden.

"Wait here a minute," he says as he jumps from the car and disappears into the hovel. Twenty infuriating minutes later, he staggers out with a shit-eating grin on his freckled dial, and his eyeballs practically hanging on his cheeks. Stoned to the bejesus belt.

"Let's go!" he says, as if he's waiting for us to get on with it.

So we finally get on the road north, with Flathead yapping like a Jack Russell terrier the whole way. Doesn't matter how loud Lychee turns up the music, he's still flapping his gums for all he's worth, and saying nothing worth a pinch of shit with any of it. Progress is irritatingly slow because Flatty is demanding that we stop at every single roadhouse so he can feed these monster munchies he's got.

A couple of hours into it, he's showing no sign of slowing down or shutting up. In fact, he's taken to amusing himself by sticking his ugly ginger scone out the window and shouting crap like "ay mate yer bumper's hangin' off" at every car we pass. So they pull over and check it out of course. Real high-brow stuff this, and of course the Flatwegian is cackling like an old chook every time he gets a car to pull over, watching 'em disappear in the wing mirror and gurgling with pleasure.

As we come up on another car, Flatty gets a brainwave. He drops his drawers and somehow twists his wiry frame so he can hang his arse out the window as we go past. Which turns out to be a bad move, because the bloke in the car reaches out his window and puts a blue flashing light on the roof. Fuck! It's a copper!

I pull over, and of course the flatfoot ignores me and goes straight for the Flathead.

"What the bloody hell do you think you're doing sonny?" asks the cop with a face like a rabid Rottweiler – if the Rottweiler was red.

"Just havin' a bit of fun mate," says Flathead, flashing a cheeky lopsided leer.

"Fun for you, disgusting and dangerous for other road users," says the cop, almost spitting with distaste – clearly he's remembering the sight of the Flatness's scabby clacker. "What would have happened if you'd scared another driver off the road with that horrible thing?" he says.

"Me arse ain't that ugly is it mate?" asks Flatty wryly, but his grin is starting to fade.

"ID thanks," says the cop. Flathead reefs into his shorts and pulls out his wallet so he can hand the bloke his licence. The copper studies it for a few seconds, then stumps off to his car to call it in.

"Shit!" says Flathead, then he says, "Quick, eat these boys," holding out a couple of pills with one hand as he pops two in his mouth with the other. Without thinking, me and Lychee drop the pills.

"Fuck, what were they?" hisses Lychee, realising what we've just done. "Just a little campfire diversion," says the knobhead with a wickedly innocent air. "The kinda shit that makes ya see meteor showers whether there's one happening or not." There's no time to discuss it though, because the cop is stumping back towards us and he has a winner's smirk on his face.

"Francis there appear to be an outstanding warrant on you, I'm going to ask you to accompany me to the police station in town," he says.

The look on Flathead's face tells me he knew this was going to happen as soon as he saw the cop going off to radio in. The cop looks at me and says, "You can follow me to town if you'd care to collect your mate when I'm done with him." Flatty follows him to the cop car and they get in, and we all head off to town. At least it's further up the road in the right direction.

By the time we pull into Wakanobbin an hour later, I'm having serious trouble driving. The eccy has come on in a big way, Lychee has Slipknot wound up to 12 on the stereo and a dreamy, faraway look on his face, and in between songs he talks about how much he likes rooting.

All I want to do is stare at the rainbow of colours the afternoon sun is washing over the landscape, and I feel like telling Lychee that he reminds me of a big teddy bear who needs a hug. I wonder how the hell Flatty is going up ahead, sitting in a cop car with a cop and a fierce E spin going on in his already pretty fucked-up head.

I cautiously pull up behind the cop car outside the station and we get out, keeping our distance. Lychee's eyes look like big black golf balls and we're both grinding our teeth like we're milling iron ore in there. Flathead jumps out of the cop car and waves happily, calling out, "This'll only take an hour or so boys, meet youse at the pub!"

He follows the cop into the station, and there's nothing for it but for the two of us to head to the pub and await the result.

The Wakanobbin Hotel is your standard country pub — creaky old wooden floors, magnificent hardwood bar behind which stands a massive-breasted matronly woman of around 60, and a crew of wild-eyed throwbacks getting shitfaced and looking for someone to fight later.

Lychee and I walk into this bastion of riding boots, red dust and lurking malevolence, cacking ourselves at Flathead's foibles. And we stop dead. For about thirty seconds you could hear a pin drop as every one of these products of the shallow end of the gene pool looks at us as if we're the freaks.

The menace in the room harshes our mellow for a minute, but we remember we're on planet pluto and stop caring, flash a big cheesy smile at everyone and breast the bar, staring straight at the barmaid's massive melons. As we order a couple of beers, the locals go back to what they were doing, which is drinking gloomily and not saying much. But you can tell that they all feel violated, and that they may do a little violatin' of their own later if they get the opportunity.

We settle in at the bar with our beers, trying fruitlessly to keep the conversation down to a dull roar and covering topics that I can distantly divine are way too bizarre for the backwoods weirdos surrounding us. Maybe because we're just gibbering, after a while they seem to forget we're there and we carry on tripping and drinking.

Five or six beers go down the hatch and we're feeling mighty chipper, when in bowls the Flatasaurus, laughing like a drain and whooping like a siren.

The locals shake their heads at this new monstrosity, but they're all pretty wasted by now, so it's about all they can do to lift their misshapen heads off the bar.

In a loud voice punctuated by plenty of "fucks" and "motherfuckers", Flatty explains his afternoon. It seems he's had a long, deep and very meaningful conversation with the plod on the way back to the cop shop, which ended with him claiming, with sincerity and massively dilated pupils, to have seen the error of his ways.

The cop has agreed to let him continue on his surfing trip with his friends, who both have actual jobs and are upright citizens, as long as he fronts his own local cop shop in a couple of days. The reason the whole thing took so long was that the cop insisted that "poor Francis" accompany him home, where Mrs Fuzz cooked him a great big steak and watched him eat it before the plod drove him back to the pub.

Flathead belches with content and skulls his second beer in three minutes. You gotta admit, the boy's got some style.

We hang out at the pub till about half an hour before stumps, figuring it wise to clear out of town before any of the local punters can invite us to witness their pugilistic prowess up close and personal.

Lucky for me, the cop has gone to bed early, figuring he's done his good deed for the day, because in my outrageously illegal condition I can barely see the road. The only thing I have on my side is that I don't exceed ten kilometres an hour the whole way to the next roadside parking bay.

Lychee and I sleep in the car, all bent into strange and uncomfortable shapes, while Flathead rolls his sleeping bag out in the dirt and sings himself to sleep, satisfied with the day's events.

At 5.30am he's rapping hard on the car window, desperate to get on the road. My sleep has been fitful, to say the least – Lychee has been dropping the most horrific psychedelically textured lager bombs all night, and occasionally howling in his sleep, and I've awoken with a foul beer and eccy hangover, coupled with a neck so stiff I can barely move. I growl at Flathead, but I'm awake now, so I open up, get out and stretch.

"C'mon Dude!" says the Flatman, "we've got a lotta miles to cover."

"Yeah I know," I reply, "it's like two hours from here."

"Um, actually it's a bit longer ay," he says artlessly. "We just gotta go back to where we were stopped. I kinda chucked a bag of weed in the bush."

Holy shit! I didn't see him do it, and neither did Lychee. And neither, clearly, did the cop. We stop at the roadhouse to fill up and scoff a rancid sausage and egg muffin washed down with an iced coffee, then we're back on the road heading in the wrong direction again.

We finally locate the tyre marks that show where we stopped behind the cop's car and pull in there again. After twenty minutes of scrabbling around in the bush Flatarse announces "got it!" and Lychee and I give each other that look again. The bloke is amazing. Before we can get back on the tar though, Flatty's gotta scuttle off into the bush "to back one out".

Almost four hours, two hot dogs, three piss stops and a Bob Marley spliff later, we roll up in the camping area overlooking the point. The deserted, tiny, blown out, what-fucking-surf point. There's an old wizened acid casualty sitting in front of his ragged tent – the only one left in this flyblown wind tunnel – and he chortles when he hears us swearing.

"Shoulda been here this morning boys, it was fuckin' all time. Nearly as good as yesterday arvo eh?" he wheezes as he rolls a durry.

Like I said, I'm never going on a surf trip with Flathead again. At least not till next time he asks.

The Ride

What could have happened.

It felt like he was flying. The wind was whipping through his hair at warp speed, and the drops of spray being torn off the face of the wave were tiny stinging bullets. The thing stood up in front of him like the blade of an impossibly long, tall, wide bulldozer, steel grey-green, and curling all down the line.

Race me, it said, and Kade needed no second invitation. He bobbed and weaved, stretched and compressed with all the speedy grace he could muster, and outran the foaming chaos behind him.

Still it grew in front of him, the curl of the blade growing more and more pronounced until at last it threw right over him, and he was standing inside the spinning green apocalypse. Fuck, it was beautiful. The just-risen sun was a few degrees off to his right, behind the glass curtain, and with every millisecond the light grew more golden and the wall became a lighter orange-green. He stood still inside it for as long as he could, but then the tunnel pinched and receded, the back of his board was pitched up by the foamball, and he was thrown headlong into the whirling swirl.

Popping up, he jumped back on his board and started the long paddle back up to the point. Fuck he'd come a long way – easily the furthest he'd ever come at Balangan.

He loved the place.

There was so much that was perfect about it – the white beach, the sweeping curve of the bay and the gnarled majesty of the headland at its western end. The way the waves looked, every one of them, so dreamily flawless.

But there was also much that was hard, or annoying, or deceptive about it, too – the crazy crowds and the terrible traffic they caused in the water, the jagged bitch of a reef, the shocking ratio of closeouts to makeable waves.

Rides like the one he'd just had were as rare as rocking-horse shit, and as prized as unicorn tears. But the possibility of snagging one, the mere suggestion that it could happen in spite of all the obstacles, kept him coming back.

Take this morning, for instance.

From the second he'd woken up he'd had a feeling that today was going to be his day. He'd picked his way out to the headland on the bottom of the tide, humming and grinning all the way, and timed his jump off carefully. A set appeared out of the pre-dawn darkness and thumped him, dragging him down the bay a ways. At last, after no less than seven waves, it had relented, and he'd paddled back to the point, already weary.

Balangan wasn't done extracting dues just yet, though. For the next half an hour, every five minutes a new and bigger set broke fifty metres or more further out than the last, so he spent his whole time duck-diving, getting worked, and paddling like a bastard to try and beat the next one.

Finally, an energy-sapping forty minutes after jumping off the dry reef, he was sitting way, way out to sea off the point – so far out he could take the whole headland and bay in at one short, sweeping glance – gathering his breath and trying to conquer his growing nervousness.

And then the wave had come, and he was all alone with the ocean, and he took it and he made it. And now he was paddling back out, telling himself that a man could die happy after a wave like that. But he wanted another one anyway. That feeling that it was going to be his day had come true.

What actually happened.

It felt like he was flying. The wind was whipping through his hair at what felt like warp speed, and the drops of rain that were no more than a drizzle were hitting his face like tiny stinging bullets.

He'd had a feeling that today was going to be his day, and he'd gone at it full steam. But the few seconds that he'd saved by not putting on his bike helmet – fuck, it wasn't as if the Bali cops cared – put him on that sharp right hand corner near Warung Susuke on Jalan Pantai Balangan, fifty metres ahead of where he would otherwise have been. And his wild self-assurance had him going into it faster and deeper than he might otherwise have done. At precisely the same time as the water truck from the Aman Gati Hotel was coming the other way, lumbering wide around the corner.

He was never going to get out of its way in time, and in his last moments he thought of those few he'd seconds saved by not putting on the helmet.

Traffic was held up for thirty minutes while they scooped his brains off the road. It had been his day after all.

We three

I found her at Balangan.

I'd sailed up the Western Australian coast on the 67 foot yacht that I'd 'liberated', stopping at every port to stock up and search for other survivors. Everywhere I went I was met with the stench of death and the howl of loneliness, and found no other living person. The only thing that kept me sane was the regular surf stops along the way.

When I made Bali, I dropped anchor in Jimbaran Bay and spent the afternoon in the crow's nest, scanning the island for evidence of human life. Months had passed since the wipeout, and I could see the signs of furious growth on the green island, already healing the scars of civilisation. There were more birds in the air, and fish, turtles, even dugongs in the clear waters, than I'd ever seen.

Next morning, I thought I might take the tender up to Uluwatu for a look and maybe a surf. If that wasn't to my liking, I could meander back via Padang Padang, Impossibles and Bingin. But as I passed Balangan I noticed a column of dark smoke rising up from the grazing land at the top of the cliff that hangs like doom over the beach. I stopped the boat and watched. The colour, density and volume of smoke were identical to those of any of the thousands of rubbish burn-offs I'd seen on the Bali coast over many years – thick, possibly toxic and obviously confined to a well-ordered pile.

I set about securing the tender outside the surf line. The breeze was almost non-existent, the ocean was that wonderful oily glass consistency that makes the best Bali days so perfect, and a four foot swell was running.

It was hard to see from the back of the waves how big they really were or how well they were breaking, but my objective was to get to shore, so I wasn't concerned about the surf anyway.

While I was doing this, I watched the dogs on the beach playing, scavenging for food and sleeping. And that's when I saw her. She ran down the front steps at the Point Hotel, right under the lee of the headland, with a board under her arm, and started picking her way across the reef. I grabbed my board and paddled towards her, and waited in the takeoff zone.

She was breathless when she made it out to where I was, partly from the exertion and partly from the excitement. She was trembling. "You're alive," she said between gasps of breath.

"You too," I said with a broad grin.

"Are you alone?" she asked. I nodded.

"Are you?"

She nodded.

"Gone. All gone," she said.

She was naturally gorgeous, probably a few years younger than me, and spoke English with a very slight French accent.

What are the odds, I asked myself, *of being left alone in the world in a place like this with a woman like that?*

For the next couple of hours, we surfed and talked. Neither of us had any idea why almost every other person on the planet had dropped dead within the same 24 hour period.

"Greed," she said. "Karma."

I was reluctant to admit that I was probably as greedy as anyone else who'd been alive and living in my situation, and no doubt had just as much karma stored up as any of them.

"Nature reclaiming her own," I said, and she agreed.

She told me that over many weeks, armed with only a wheelbarrow and a minivan, she'd gathered up every one of the bodies littered in and around the Balangan area – all the way up to the big Nirmala shopping centre on Jalan Uluwatu, and cremated them in massive fires. It was hard and it was awful and sickening, particularly the longer it went on, but at least she could live there knowing she'd done what she could. She'd started a vegetable garden, but she still made regular trips to the supermarkets and empty restaurants and hotel kitchens for dried and canned foods. I marvelled at her strength.

Balangan that day was the best I'd ever surfed it, lining up perfectly at a playful four foot, with some hollow sections and some fast turn opportunities. The water gleamed like crystal and the sky was a blue diamond. We talked and surfed, and I watched her decimate every wave she took. She had poise and presence, style to burn and turns to envy, and nothing seemed to ruffle her surface. She was as calm as the glassy ocean itself.

We spent the night at her place and she cooked for me, the most wonderful and fulfilling meal I'd ever eaten. I was sure I'd actually died myself, and this was heaven. We made love while the roosters crowed, the cows lowed, and the frogs hummed outside. She'd been as hungry for it as I had.

Every day for the next six or seven weeks was almost but not exactly a duplicate of the others, with subtle differences that made each a gem of its own. We surfed Balangan every day – flawless waves, sometimes smaller, some days bigger and more challenging. We had deep, honest conversations with the effervescent beauty of Bali all around us and in us. And we revelled in a happiness only lightly marred by the knowledge that we two were alone in the world.

We took the tender to Uluwatu and surfed Outside Corner together, and she was as fearless as she was skilled. I watched her thread triple overhead bombs with the same calm, easy confidence she showed when she speared a fish, milked a cow or created a Michelin-star-worthy meal.

Together we worked to grow and prepare our food, made fishing nets, ploughed the hard earth, and scouted the area between Uluwatu and Seminyak for stores and items we still needed. The days skidded by, and the nights were quietly filled with bliss and togetherness.

But there's something in a man that can't accept perfection. I still had my yacht, and I wanted her to come with me and search for others like us. She couldn't understand my need to do that. "Why?" she asked.

"To find out if we're really alone," I said.

"Does it matter? We're together."

It mattered to me. I couldn't convince her to come, but I was resolved. One dark, cloudy morning, with a light onshore breeze chopping the two foot swell into crumbling closeouts, I left her and went back to my yacht. Stopping only to restock the boat with fuel and whatever else I could find in the rotting horror of Benoa Harbour, I sailed away.

I crossed the Indian Ocean, stopping along the coast of Java and sampling the treasures of Panaitan, the Mentawai, Banyak and Telo Islands along the way. I pressed on to Nias, across to Sri Lanka and then to Madagascar and Africa, to surf and to search. Here and there I found small numbers of people alive; nowhere was I welcomed, and in most places I was threatened.

The further I went, the more I rued my decision to leave her, but the more determined I became in my quest to find…what? I had no idea. In the end, I realised that if I was searching for anything, it was what I'd already abandoned back in Balangan.

I turned east and sailed as direct a line as I could for Bali, hoping against hope that she would still be there. When after three long years of fruitless wandering I sailed into the blue-green paradise of Balangan, my heart was heavy with fear that she would be gone. Perhaps dead, possibly moved on. Maybe even with another survivor like me. Who knew?

I dropped anchor just beyond the surfline and looked, as I had done so often in so many places, for those telltale signs of human habitation. And then I saw them.

Two of them, standing on the beach waving at me. She was there, with my son.

Since that day, we've never left our bay except to surf and scavenge. We surf Balangan when it's on, and when it isn't we enjoy its beauty and its soul and each other. We've never seen anyone else, and we could not be happier.

We three.

Mundaka '93
(A true story)

We'd put away a goodly number of *cervezas* the night before, and I was feeling rather poorly when we made the morning pilgrimage to the railing by the river mouth at Mundaka on the Feast of San Jose.

Six to eight foot sets were relentlessly booming onto the shallow sand bar under a leaden sky, and there were fifteen or twenty black-clad figures on boards at the peak – at that moment scrambling to get over a particularly large and gnarly beast. It looked like it was getting bigger by the minute.

I ran back to the flat and put on my wetsuit, half excited, half scared to death. Mundaka was bigger, meaner and more exciting than I had yet seen it, and my nerves were jumping around like I had fleas under my skin – a feeling I relish now, but which at the time made me slightly nauseous.

On the adrenalin-charged paddle out, I held onto the wild belief that I would get the best, and probably biggest, wave of my life. Without that to spur me on, the sight of those heaving swells would have sent me scurrying back to shore without even getting my hair wet.

As I neared the peak I could see that even the mildest waves were throwing sheets of water – lips two feet thick – about three metres straight out. Giant square tubes that were dark and hollow and a beautifully dangerous place to be.

Taking off on the inside would be the act of a madman. No surprise, then, to see the American doctor we knew as *Hamus* (the Spanish pronunciation of James) dropping vertically down a twelve or thirteen foot face and outrunning the thunderous lip to take on the jacking section, his board screaming across the muddy grey water with only the tiniest sliver of the rail in the wall.

I began asking myself what the fuck I was doing there. I'd been back surfing for a bit over a year after a ten year break, practising in the minuscule, powerless waves of Cottesloe Beach, and here I was taking on mountainous, unforgiving surf in lethally cold water. Still, I tried to think brightly of what a story it would be to tell the rapt listeners back home, "Yeah, paddled out at ten foot Mundaka, slipped into a couple of double decker bus sized tubes and spent the afternoon slamming tequila to the glory of San Jose."

It sounded good to me, and sitting on the peak, the boys were all encouragement. Marty, Cam, Craig and Hamus were all there revelling in the wild conditions, taking off on waves too evil to contemplate. When a solid eight footer stood up on the bank, the fellas urged me onto it.

"Go the barrel son!" shouted Cameron as I jettisoned all sense of reason and paddled into the rising beast. The water at the base of the wave was getting shallower and further away with every quickened beat of my heart, and pretty soon I was beyond the point of no return. Even to ditch at this stage would be tantamount to suicide. Luckily, I was running out of time to think, as a jump in speed and a drop in elevation told me I was now one with the wave and going where it went. I got to my feet, numb with terror and elation.

"Jesus, the size of it," I was thinking as the top of the wave disappeared skywards.

Suddenly I was at full stretch, my board dropping away beneath me like an express elevator, my heart leaving little dents on the inside of the top of my head. Down I went into the depths of the wave, reaching the bottom to find that, miraculously, the board was still under me. I'd made the drop. This scared the shit out of me.

I had no option but to ride the bastard then – and the next bit was an almighty jacking section. I was about to pick up some serious speed, and I was already going faster than my thoughts could keep up. The bottom turn was life or death, a steep lean at a mad angle to heave the thing around to face the wall, and somehow I pulled it off.

The intensity of the acceleration, the insane sensation of gathering thrust as my board streaked across a solid wall of water well over twice my height and a million times my weight, is with me now as I write – my hands are sweaty and my heart thumps faster as I relive that frantic ride.

I took the high line through the jack-up, blissed out to see that the lip wasn't going to outrun me. I was through the hell section, so I settled a bit, leaning back a touch to slow the board, and sticking the tips of my fingers into the towering hill of water that raced past beside me. I crouched, although I couldn't have touched the top of the thing if I was standing on my tiptoes with my arms outstretched, and the tube overtook me, enveloping me in its misty timelessness.

For what seemed like ages I studied the classic tube-view – the messy river-ocean water fell in a shattering of cloudy crystal on my right, and I could see the emerald green of the hill on the other side of the river framed by the tunnel of water I was in. I leaned forward just a speck and shot out of the cylinder, admiring my courage and style as much as the now manageable head-and-a-half high wave that walled off into the distance. The feeling was upon me: I was invincible, a champion. A god.

"Now for a reo," I said to myself in triumph. Fool. I turned down to the bottom of the wave and aimed back up for a section of the lip about five board lengths away. Now, I'd been told the golden rule of Mundaka many times, broken it before, and suffered the consequences. But I did it again. Attempted a re-entry in a place where the lip is not accepting of that kind of audacity. Unless the tide is way in and the wave is as fat as your grandmother, Mundaka will not allow a successful reo, and it will punish you for trying same.

The meat of my board struck the lip just as it began to throw its numberless tendrils shorewards, and my board and rag-doll-like self were unceremoniously lip-launched into space. Thrown bodily off the wave and pummelled into the sand for my insolence.

How quickly and profoundly the mighty did fall. How swiftly the warm glow of self-admiration gave way to the chill horror of an Atlantic Ocean thrashing.

I surfaced, sputtering and freezing, in time to see a wave about the same size preparing to smack me on the head. I dived under it, hoping my legrope would hold against the vast weight of the roiling white water. I was hauled along backwards underwater at a speedy pace, and when I came up I saw I'd been pulled into the path of yet another aquatic fiend that loomed above my head like some ungodly predator, ready to swallow me whole.

Again I dived, again I came up to another set wave. I was staring hell in the face when I came up yet again to find another one of the bastards poised to crush me. But the set couldn't last forever, and a brief lull before the next one was all I needed to grab my 6'7" and jump on in time to paddle over it.

I was fucked! And I had to paddle around three hundred energy-sapping metres back to the peak. But by the time I got there I was grinning, raving about the wave I'd got, and laughing about being lip-launched yet again. The paddle out had even warmed me up a bit, but it was still fairly arctic out there, so I didn't want to sit around. I was hanging out to take another wave.

A hulking seven footer with a face like a junkyard dog and a similar attitude stalked in from the open ocean and I turned to paddle for it, my confidence soaring. It stood up straighter than I expected, and as soon as I took my feet, I knew I was doomed. There were ledges and boils all over its snarling face, and its fearsome peak was foaming rabidly. The wave went beyond vertical while I was still hovering at the top, and I went backwards over the edge in a pall of terror. Down I went, like a bag of shit, and hit the cold water.

The lip came down immediately behind me, and threw its

massive weight right into the pit of my stomach, driving me into the sandy bottom as easily as I would crush a bug under my heel.

I was held to the bottom, paralysed by the mass of water pinning me there and the sheer blackness, for what seemed to be the equivalent of a short lifetime. Then, as the wave passed over me, it lifted me up and shook me with a savagery I'd not encountered in all the horrible wipeouts I'd had there. After several eternities underwater, being flayed and wrung out properly, I surfaced, bursting for want of air.

The first thing I noticed was my mate Marty's face. But it seemed small, distant. It was. He was perched right at the top of a two storey building made of icy, hard Atlantic water, about to topple over just a couple of metres away. Marty wisely pulled out, but I had no choice. I dived under the monster as it broke with almighty fury in about two feet of water. The explosion was excruciating, and the onset of the thrashing so severe that I was considering saying my prayers and kissing the world goodbye. But instead of carrying me with it, the wave shoved me out the back with contempt, and as the hellion receded behind me, I gulped down lungfuls of delicious air.

The next wave was advancing rapidly, my board was a long way away at the end of a seriously stretched legrope, and I told myself that this, at last, was it. As the mound of freezing water moved in to claim my exhausted body, adrenaline accomplished what my sagging will had insisted was impossible. In a flash I heaved on my legrope, grabbed the board and paddled over the top of the wave before it broke.

I had been certain that it was the last thing I'd ever see on this blue earth, and I was so stoked when I actually made it over the top that I let out a whoop. I sat out the back panting.

Marty was almost hysterical with laughter.

"Fuck mate, did you cop that on the head or what?" he cackled. "I looked over the top, and all I could see was this little black dot – that's your head – right in the path of the lip. Fuck that must have hurt! A good solid ten footer that one, too. Shit that was funny." Marty laughed like a drain and carried on in a similar vein while I smiled thinly and pondered the imminent abbreviation of my life, probably by the next set.

The set, when it came, looked manageable at six or seven foot, so I took the second one, after watching Cameron safely take the drop and disappear, hooting, into the bowl.

As I paddled, I recalled Cam's advice: always put in two or three extra strokes, even when you're sure you're on the wave. It was good advice, and for once I followed it. The drop was sweet, the set up spectacular and the tube a glimpse of infinity.

I rode the rolling, thundering beast all the way to the close-out and flicked off. Didn't even have to deal with the wave behind – just paddled straight over it and headed out to the distant peak.

I was recovering from the foul bashing I'd had before, and as I sat out the back it came to me that no one would notice if I took the six and seven footers and judiciously left the eight, nine and increasingly frequent ten footers that were charging across the ocean to slam onto the sandbank. God, that hollow boom can sound so sickening when it's unleashed just a few metres away. But shit it sounds sweet when it's behind you and you're about to stall into the cavern it creates.

After about an hour of riding some of the best waves of my life, fear began to creep into the equation again. The smaller waves were becoming fewer and further between, and they were breaking so far in that if I paddled for one and missed it, I'd almost certainly cop a repeat of the earlier thumping, only this time probably on a bigger wave and a shallower sandbar.

I watched as the waves grew in height and thickness, and my terror escalated accordingly. The sets travelled in groups of about eight, with each successive wave getting bigger until the last of the set was beyond my ability to contemplate its size. The second or third wave of the set, at about eight to ten feet, would have to be the one. That was bigger than I cared to ride, but I was running out of choices and the swell kept growing.

I told myself these apartment-block sized bits of water were only water, and reasoned that I'd already survived some evil workings – was almost used to them in fact – so if I happened to be on the receiving end of yet another demented beating, I'd at least be on familiar territory. I also told myself it was better to die like a man than to paddle in like a chicken.

I identified the set a couple of minutes before it arrived – when the swell has that much size and definition you can see a set from the time it strikes the island a couple of kilometres away – and set my mind to taking the third wave. It would probably be pushing around ten feet by the time it got to us, but I remained calm and focussed, "facing death with zen-like indifference", as I later explained over a welcome *caña* in the Bar Portubide.

Breathing deeply, I watched the wave sweeping in like a silent assassin. I took off closer to the shoulder than the inside of the peak, which made the drop easier to handle but left precious little time to set up for the critical section. The launch was an intense, action packed event. A fiercely steep descent followed by a desperate bottom turn and a climb almost to the lip, to glide through the jacking section at warp speed.

This set me up for far and away the biggest, roundest and most wondrous tube I've ever been embraced by. As I shot out of the tube, still way overhead and charging like a bull elephant, my trailing left hand snagged a lump on the face. I lurched forward and overbalanced by an eighth of a thousandth of a millimetre, stayed glued to the wildly bucking board for a nanosecond, and was then catapulted across the black granite wall. I went up and over with the lip and was drilled heavily into the sand, rolling and spinning in the maelstrom, being torn limb from limb, it seemed.

Inside the seething viciousness, my left bootie was ripped out from under my wetsuit and torn three quarters of the way off my foot. Near-freezing water started filling my wetsuit, fuelling my panic.

Surfacing a few seconds later, I was thrilled to see my board floating just inches away. I grabbed it and got on, and let the next wave wash over me. Exhaustion mingled with the unbelievable cold of the water filling my wetsuit, so I let the next couple of waves roll over me and push me towards shore. I happily accepted the two small poundings that accompanied this event, as they drove me down into the river proper so I could paddle straight into the port. Looking up, I could see the railing crowded with people watching the mayhem on the peak. "Good," I thought. "If I freeze to death right here, they'll notice me and send a rescue boat."

The paddle into the chill brown water of the port was agony. My leg was numb from the ice seeping in through the gap at my foot, but at last I crawled up the slimy port steps and sat down to pull my boot back on. I walked slowly back to our flat. I considered Mundaka and me to be even: she had both frightened and beaten the shit out of me, but I had taken some of her treasures for my own.

Mundaka 2029

"Jeez, this place looks a bit bloody different! Where's all the colourful bars, the flags, the people?" thought Louie Lasarte as the taxi pulled up in a narrow cobbled street hemmed in by dim grey walls, and not a sign of life anywhere. "*Aqui*," said the taxi driver.

"Here?" asked Louie in English.

"*Si. Setenta euros*," replied the driver seriously, completely expressionless. Louie paid the 70 euros and struggled to get his bulky double board bag out of the back of the Seat wagon while the driver watched, shaking his head. With the board bag and his luggage, Louie was fully laden, and he had no idea which one of the blank walls and doors that faced the street might be his cousin Jojo's. He wasn't even sure that the taxi driver had dropped him in the right street, the place had changed so much.

He wandered up and down for a few minutes and at last found the familiar heavy green door of his cousin's house. He knocked, and in a few seconds his cousin Jojo opened it warily. They hadn't seen each other since Louie' last visit, but instead of being pleased to see him, Jojo cast an anxious look at the board bag, quickly scanned the street, and hustled Louie inside. "Shit! I knew you'd bring your boards!" he said. He sounded panicky.

"Mate, what's the problem?" asked Louie. He walked into the kitchen and started casually fishing around in his cousin's cupboards, hunting for the block of hash he knew would be there somewhere. He was ready for a relaxing buzz.

"There's been a crackdown. No more surfing," said Jojo.

"You're fucking kidding!" Louie had travelled all the way from Australia to the nether regions of the Basque country to go surfing, and here was Jojo trying to tell him he couldn't!

"How? Why? They can't just stop you from going surfing can they?"

"Ah, *mi amigo*, you Southern Hemisphere types have it so good you don't even know it. Think yourself lucky that the new fascism hasn't taken over Australia yet. In the last few years the right wing has been getting stronger and stronger here in Europe, starting with demonstrations and riots to stop the flow of refugees they call immigrants. Then after the fascists won the election in France in 2027, it was inevitable that they would start to move on the rest of Europe.

"We're next door to France, so we were among the first to fall under the jackboot. Now the right – *Derecho* – is in charge here, and they can do whatever they like. Especially members of the Party. When was the last time you were here, five years ago? It was paradise then, compared to now."

"I could see that things had changed when I got off the

train in Gernika, but I thought it was just winter dullness. And anyway, even if the fascists are making bigger pricks of themselves than they were before, why would they ban surfing here at Mundaka? It's the best left in the northern hemisphere.

"I mean, they were running around with their idiotic banners, starting fights and pretty much being nazis the last time I was here, but we were allowed to surf then. So why not now?" As he spoke, he waved a lighter flame under the brown block of hash, crumbling it into a cigarette paper already covered with a small pile of crushed tobacco.

"They were just trouble-makers then, but they're in charge now," said Jojo. "And recently the party opened up a barracks for the *Derecho Juventud* – you know, the kids who all look and behave like perfect Aryans. They decided to teach them to surf, to develop a kind of surf warfare. So they closed the break to us. The *Derecho Juventud* get to surf, and we get to watch.

"These kids are like gods – their fathers and uncles are all in positions of power in the party, and they're ruthless." Jojo's tone was one of bitter resignation, and Louie shook his head, making the black beanie that covered it bounce around like a squash ball.

"Fuck, they're not kidding when they call these guys fascist assholes, are they?" he said.

"Please," said Jojo. "Don't talk about the Party like that – you never know who's listening. Just accept that we can't surf here any more. We can always go down to *Bakio* or up to *Laga*. There are other breaks we can surf."

"That's fucking ridiculous! Couldn't we, you know, paddle out and kind of mingle with the Hitler kiddies?" Louie asked. Jojo was watching mesmerised as Louie deftly twitched up the hash joint, his own lip twitching with every sneering word about the *Derecho*.

"No way," said Jojo. "The *Juventud* have boards and wetsuits marked with stylised swastikas, and they carry weapons in the water as part of their training. You'd be spotted – and eliminated – before you ever got to the lineup."

Louie held his joint up proudly. "The hash is still ok though?" he asked with a grin.

"Oh yeah," his cousin replied, pleased to change the subject from the Party and the *Derecho Juventud*. "It keeps us quiet and compliant, so they're happy for us to keep on smoking," he said as Louie lit up. They smoked awhile without speaking, grunting to each other to take the joint when it was time.

"I can't believe it. They banned surfing at Mundaka," Louie said quietly, breaking the long silence.

"And at most of the decent spots up the coast too," Jojo said, as quietly. "Hossegor, Biarritz, Lacanau – all closed to the locals, open only to the party. Even down in Portugal there are hardly any spots where you're allowed to go out."

"All that coast and no surfing."

"It's been going off too," said Jojo.

"Ah, don't tell me mate! I brought these boards all this way for nothin'." He put his head in his hands, realised that he was still wearing his beanie and took it off, letting long blonde hair fall across his face.

"*La mierda de la puta*!" yelped Jojo. "Did anyone else see that?" he asked urgently. "The customs guy, the people in the airport, the taxi driver???"

"See what?"

"Your hair! Your blonde hair! It makes you a target! Did anyone see it?"

"Nah, I always tuck it up under my beanie when I go through customs mate – if they it see I usually get taken straight to the ol' rubber glove room. I s'pose I've just left it there when I trained it to Gernika and then got a taxi here." Louie was far less concerned than Jojo, but then, he wasn't armed with the same rumours and fears as his cousins.

"If they catch you – a big, healthy man with blue eyes and blonde hair, they'll take you away in a flash," said Jojo.

"Who'll take me away, and where?" Louie was becoming irritated with his cousin's paranoia.

"The *fascismo* of course!" hissed Jojo. "You must remember, you're not in Australia anymore, you're in Spain. Fascist Spain. And you look and act like a pure aryan but you're not in the party. They'll take you wherever it is they take people like you. Rumour has it that they attach a catheter to you and suck out your sperm for a couple of months, for impregnating perfect aryan females, then they kill you and feed your brains and liver to the *Derecho Juventud* to give them strength and courage. Whatever the real truth is, you don't want to know it – so that hair is coming off tonight!"

Louie was less convinced by his cousin's words than he was by the tone of his voice – it had a pitch of raw terror about it – and he immediately consented to a head shave. Jojo ferreted around in the kitchen and came up with some clippers, and a short while later all that remained of Louie's treasured locks was a pile of golden rubbish on the floor. Thankfully his roots had been reasonably dark, so he no longer looked blonde. In fact, he looked a bit pasty, which was ideal.

"The thing to do," said Jojo, "is to walk with a stoop if you can, especially if you see anyone in any uniform at all; police,

Derecho SS or *Gestapo*, soldiers, *Derecho Juventud*, anyone with a swastika. You must learn not to be noticed. And if you are noticed, play up your Australianness. Blame your ignorance for any transgressions, but for God's sake be meek! Otherwise you just don't know where you'll end up."

"Yeah, got it," said Louie absently, stoned, tired and beyond taking in any more bad news. "Tell you the truth mate, I've been in the air, on trains and in taxis since some time a couple of days ago, and I'm rooted, and that hash is bloody excellent. If you don't mind, I think I need some sleep."

The next morning, Jojo and Louie took the short walk through the small town to the little port holding a couple of dozen sardine fishers. Over the sea wall at the port there lay the wide, sandy rivermouth, and beyond it the Atlantic Ocean. They walked along the sea wall, watching the waves break on the sand bar that almost covered the entire river mouth.

At this time of year there was a narrow channel, maybe ten metres wide, through which river flowed, running rapidly past the wall on which they stood. Vast, perfect six footers peeled endlessly on the sandbar, flaunting massive empty barrels. Louie was itching to get out there. "Man, there's no one out!" he said. "And look at that! If you took off now you'd get a fuckin' forty second tube! Why don't we just paddle out and surf till the little Hitler bastards come out?"

Jojo looked around furtively. "Shhh!" he hissed. "Don't even say that stuff. They'll shoot you just for thinking of going out, and I shudder to think what they'd do if they heard you describe the *Derecho Juventud* like that! It's their break now, and that's all there is to it. They go out for two hours every morning and afternoon regardless of the conditions, and they'll be going off today. If you like we can sit and watch — it's good form to watch and applaud anyway — or we could sit inside and get stoned."

"Let's get stoned here and watch the miserable little shits," said Louie, producing a joint he'd already rolled.

"Don't call them that for christ's sake. You'll get us both shot!"

At precisely ten am, a squad of wetsuit-clad *Derecho Juventud* jogged down the short path from their barracks, sleek black surfboards under their arms and evil-looking weapons strapped to their sides. They stopped on the sea wall just a few metres from where Louie and Jojo sat smoking a hash joint, seemingly invisible to these rigid zealots.

Twelve of the strapping blonde youth lined up on the sea wall and, shouting *"Heil Hitler"* in unison, threw themselves into the cold water as one. They paddled in formation as the current swept them towards the clean, green peak.

As they paddled by below, Louie could see that each had a blood red Nazi eagle on the back of his wetsuit and swastikas on the arms, plus a large knife strapped to his left calf. The weapons they had strapped on were specially developed automatics designed to work wet or dry, and with which the *Juventud* showed awesome familiarity. As Louie found out over the next two hours. They might be fascist turds, but by Christ those kids could surf. And in such a bizarre, unsurflike way.

If, for instance, one of them got a tube, it was considered perfectly normal to take aim and fire his gun out of the open ended cylinder — and on that particular day, gunfire rang out constantly as the boys all got massive tubes. Dropping in on a fellow *Juventud* was an invitation for him to leap off his board, knife drawn, and attempt to gut the offender, while the disappointment of missing a wave was often expressed by tossing a grenade from the shoulder into the barrel. Louie was glad he wasn't out there – it looked particularly dangerous, and had none of the calming, cleansing qualities of free surfing. It was all about naked aggression. By the time they paddled in, in formation, exactly two hours later, Louie was stunned into silence. Say what you like about these guys, they were great surfers – strong, agile, completely fearless, and skilled enough to literally take aim and fire an automatic weapon from the inside of a barrel.

Of course, Louie was also fully amped to get out there amongst the waves, which would remain unridden until exactly 2.00pm, when the next squad would go out for their two hours. But he now understood just how harmful to his health that would be, so he retired to the bar *El Puerto* with Jojo for a long glass of *patxaran* to calm his troubled nerves.

Day after day, Louie and Jojo watched as mindless barrels rolled and spat and chewed for hour after hour. Twice a day the *Juventud* paddled out and turned surfing into some kind of martial ballet.

Occasionally the conditions turned to shit or the swell dropped – the kids went out regardless – but most of the time, perfect waves remained maddeningly unridden.

And didn't they beckon Louie! Unused to oppression as he was, unlike Jojo, he found it desperately hard to watch as wave after wave presented his vision of paradise, so easily within reach yet so far beyond his grasp.

Eventually, he couldn't go waterside at all any more, and spent most of his time sitting in Jojo's cramped living room, rolling hash joints and becoming more and more depressed.

One night, a clear, cloudless night presided over by a huge, bright full moon, Louie roused himself from the flat and hit the *Portubide* for quite a few too many *cañas* at the bar. Around midnight, he staggered over to the river's edge to gaze at the surf. Perfection thundered onto the sandbar, plain as day in the strong moonlight.

Seized by a sudden idea, Louie looked up the hill towards the *Derecho Juventud* barracks. Dark. They were all asleep, by the looks. And most of the people in town would be likewise asleep or drinking heavily in one of the bars. Quickly, quietly, Louie ran up to Jojo's, slipped into his wetsuit and grabbed his board.

He knew it was dangerous to surf in such an inebriated state, but the need to get into the waves was overwhelming. He didn't see anyone as he stole across town and slid silently into the grimy waters of the port.

Bitterly cold and brackish, the water tasted sweet to Louie as he paddled into the current that would take him out to the break. The moonlight played on the heaving swell, swirling and distorting the tall, silvery faces of the waves. By the time he reached the peak, he was breathing heavily with exertion and an alcohol-fuelled fear at being on such a potent piece of water in the dark.

He sat on his board, breathing deeply to calm himself and psych up for his first real wave in weeks. A dark shape loomed out of the ocean before him, and he turned and paddled across to position himself for the takeoff. He couldn't see the wave properly, nor did he notice a tiny red pinpoint of light as it fixed itself immovably on his forehead. He felt the bullet that pierced his skull and shattered his brain for only the briefest of moments. A couple of seconds later the cracking sound arrived and faded, and then it was over.

Next morning Jojo, like all of the villagers, looked blankly at the corpse displayed in the middle of the town square, and turned to the *fascismo* standing next to it. "Any idea who that was?" he asked as carelessly as possible.

"No," replied the *Derecho SS* man. And Jojo walked away, whistling in the sunshine.

The Drop In

"Bugger." Grayton Whyte knew as soon as he turned into the carpark that he wouldn't be surfing Saturation Point that day. The vehicles jammed into every available spot, sprawling over kerbs and spreading over grassy patches, told him the entire bay would be crawling with competition. Its sparkling waters would be alive with odious people, scrambling and hassling for waves, and yelling short words and long, uncomplimentary descriptions at each other. Making what should be a pleasant respite from the landlocked world a vicious shitfight. He was too old and not nearly angry enough for that any more. So he muttered, "Bugger," and swung the car around.

The other beaches and headlands would be the same. There was gorgeous, gleaming sunshine, gentle offshore breezes, and a healthy ground swell. The kind of day that brought out the blow-ins, the beginners, the mugs and kooks, and even the most casual and uncommitted weekend warriors. And that's on top of the diehards who surf every day no matter what.

There was, he knew, only one choice left. Dread Cove. Tucked away on a secret break that few people knew about and even fewer cared to surf, he'd probably paddle out into a small, hard core crowd. The quality wouldn't be what it was at Saturation Point, of course. And he dreaded the treacherous jump off from jagged, pitted rocks. But he just couldn't deal with the crowds, and at Dread Cove with only a few out he could surf relatively unmolested.

Unless He was there. The Drop In, as he was called by everyone who knew him. A big, ugly, fearless, fearsome bastard he was, and arrogant with it. Grayton had only ever seen him there twice, and both times the prick had done what his name suggested, and dropped in on a wave Grayton was already surfing.

Just as casual as you like, he'd taken possession of the wave, lazily turning to look Grayton in the eye and grin nastily at him, then carried on down the face with an air of disdain. There was malevolence in that stare though, and something of a challenge. As though he'd plainly said, "My wave. Wanna do anything about it? Because if ya do, I'll have ya!"

Both times it had happened, Grayton had been so unnerved, he'd just straightened out in the foam and gone straight in. He didn't want to tangle with the big guy in the lineup. He knew that if he paddled back out there, the brute would have turned on him just for the sheer, bloody-minded pleasure of it, and he would have been lucky to get out of it alive. Grayton told himself he wasn't just being dramatic; the Drop In really was that much of a mean, even a cruel and sadistic bastard.

Of course, Grayton hated the fear the Drop In instilled in him. The sense of intimidation and frustration that this one bloke could so imperiously rule the break. The crushing weight of the knowledge that he considered Grayton – and anyone else who dared to paddle out – so insignificant that he could sneeringly take control of any wave that he wanted. The dismay of knowing that *he knew* that Grayton would bend to his will.

There was a chance that He wouldn't be there though. That Grayton and just a couple of others would be able to share the surf evenly, without the gnawing sense of fear that the Drop In brought with him. Because if he showed up, everyone in the lineup felt it, and nobody really wanted to stay out there.

Some did, of course, out of a sort of misplaced machismo or bravado or something. But everyone who did kept a wary eye on the Drop In, and hoped like hell that he wouldn't single them out. Should they catch his eye, or worse, get in his way, even the bravest of them ended up on the beach pretty smartly. Such was the power of the bloke.

But there was always a chance that he wouldn't be there, that he'd be off hunting somewhere else. So Grayton endured the forty minutes of four-wheel drive hell that took him to Dread Cove on the off-chance that he'd be able to have a quiet surf.

"Strewth." Finding no one in the car park at the Point was a happy surprise. He thought for sure that there'd be at least a few in the water on such a crystal invitation of a day. He looked down the steep hill at the breaking point. Head high plus, clean water as clear and empty as you could ever want or imagine. Most important, no sign of the Drop In. Just a couple of seabirds squawking on the rocks above the waterline, and the point rolling along in mechanical beauty. Possibly the best he'd ever seen it.

Grayton was out of his car and into his wetsuit in a flash, agitated with the need to get into the surf before it faded, or the breeze turned, or the crowd arrived. All thoughts of the Drop In were banished, flushed away by the vision of excellent waves and no people. It was to be just him and the waves, and the wheeling, occasionally diving seabirds and the darting fish they were after.

Jumping off the rocks was hairy. A finger of razor-sharp limestone, the sharply serrated remnant of an ancient reef given voracious teeth by time and the action of ceaseless wind and waves, was the only entry point. Timing his leap was critical; an error would mean getting rolled and quite possibly coming away with shredded flesh and a trashed board. Either of which would end the surf before it started.

He almost blew the jump, and thought for a second that the wave that suddenly jacked from out of nowhere would drag him back onto the barnacle-encrusted mineral. But he just made the duckdive, pushing through the back of the powerful little swell at the precise moment it curled and threw, so the motion of the wave actually shoved him through the back of it cleanly. Paddling like a madman, he made it out to the lineup through an incoming set and sat up to catch his breath. It was bigger than it looked from the car park. The breeze was a friendly offshore, and the solitude was delicious.

A wave rose, dark and green against the weedy, reedy rocks below. Grayton turned to stroke into it. Lifting, moving forward with it, he felt its power. The drop was sweet, the bowl was sweeter. He took a high line through the section, speeding across the slick surface like a barracuda, then jammed into a cutback over the sluggish deep spot and crouched for the oncoming sucky section. A thick transparent curtain magically threw itself over the top of him, and he was encased in the green amber of a flawless cylinder for a full three seconds before being shot out like a ball from a glass cannon. Then he was off the wave and paddling back out again, relishing the stoke and stoked at the day. Looking up towards the car park carved out of the bush high at the top of the hill, he thought he saw a flash of movement up there.

"Please let no one come," he said to himself. He looked at the empty line of the horizon, deep and profoundly empty. "Let no one come," he said again. "Especially the Drop In."

As soon as he was on the bubble again, another set rolled in. He took the second wave, awed by the speed and clean power of it, and totally blown away by the skill and confidence he himself was showing. It may have been the surf of his life.

Again and again as he paddled back out after yet another perfect and technically flawless wave, he looked from the car park to the ocean horizon, hoping for the magical solitude to remain unbroken, expecting it to be at any moment. Several times he thought he heard car doors slamming up on the hill, but no one came. And the surf even seemed to be picking up.

He thought of the carnage at Saturation Point – idiots dropping in, kooks ditching boards before big sets, hassles and hoots, arguments and fights. The downer that crowds created within him and cheated him of the righteous feeling surfing should give him. He couldn't believe that he'd scored the best Dread Cove ever, with not a soul about. Surely someone would turn up soon? He could handle a companion, to be honest.

After two and a half hours of almost constant paddling and surfing, Grayton's energy was on the way out. He didn't care if anyone else turned up now, anyone at all. He felt as if the Drop In wouldn't show, and if he did Grayton would just paddle in and leave the break to him. He'd started to get lazy anyway, going for big moves in stupid spots and not caring when he got smashed, and loving it when by some miracle he made them. The waves were just so perfect, just so much better than it had ever been, and still picking up. It was well over six foot now, and pumping.

A dark line grew solemnly out of the horizon, soundlessly coming at him like a ghost freight train. He turned to paddle, his mind on the wave and what he'd do with each section, plotting each turn and planning each move. In his mind, success and glory were already in the bag. He had half a mind to take this one in, but then again maybe he should stay out until someone else arrived. Waves of this rare size and quality shouldn't go unridden.

Such were the thoughts that rushed through his mind as he stroked into a late takeoff. In a moment he was on his feet, enjoying the adrenaline rush of the elevator drop down a face well over twice his own height. He set his line through the first hollow section and was about to dig in and throw a big cutty when something caught his eye. A dark shape, moving swiftly on the very edge of his vision. Indefinable, but also instantly identifiable. The Drop In.

True to his name, he was dropping in on Grayton. Taking possession of the wave as coolly, as cold-bloodedly as only he could. The thrill of fear was intense and surprisingly agonising, a physical pain that struck him in the guts. For an instant, he was paralysed, and almost fell off his board, which surely would have been fatal. As it was, the Drop In seemed to be rounding on him, turning for the attack. Although this was their third encounter, it was the first time the Drop In had turned like this, and it looked serious.

The shape of the brute was frighteningly clear in the wall of wave stretching out before Grayton. At least five metres long, greyish brown on the top half, with a white underbelly. An amazingly thick, wide, barrel of a beast streaking along just below the power centre of the swell, with no discernible movement or indication of effort at all. He was definitely turning now, his huge, bulbous anvil head swinging to face Grayton straight on, lifting through the surface as it came.

The black eye of the creature was fully beaded on him now, and Grayton was struck with numbing terror. Less than one complete second had elapsed since he'd first seen the Drop In, but an avalanche of thoughts and emotions had tumbled through his shattered mind already.

First, he wondered if he would survive the attack, and just how much of him the shark would take in that first bite. Then he wondered, terribly, whether he would simply fall off the board and present himself as a ready-made, bite-sized meal. He determined that he wouldn't, but still reckoned that his chances of living through the next twenty seconds were under fifty percent.

Next, in desperation, he tried to gauge the distance to shore, and how much closer to land a solid jump might take him. Far too risky, he decided. If he fell short he would be without the one thing that he could, conceivably, place between himself and those giant jaws: his surfboard. Ramming six feet of fibreglass and foam into the Drop In's wide maw might be the only thing that could save him. If the bastard didn't simply swallow that along with him, like a wafer with a piece of cheese.

Thoughts, or rather fleeting images of his family and friends presented themselves to his mind's eye in awful clarity, and he saw the words TRAGEDY and HERO written all in capitals on newsprint. He never could understand how being taken by a shark would make the media describe him as a hero, even though he knew it would. Probably the extra papers they'd sell telling of his brave fight against the beast, even if in reality he'd submitted like a coward and screamed like a baby. Which he was inclining towards doing.

Then, oddly, he asked himself why such a monumentally powerful regnant being – a giant white pointer, no less – had been given such a casually dismissive and demeaning nickname like 'Drop In'. It now seemed as if the indignity of such a title grated on the shark and gave it the will to attack him.

The blunted snout was almost on him, and the colossal gullet opened wide to receive him. Row upon row of piercing, pointy triangular teeth pushed closer, straining at what he could only describe as lips, and he knew the time for reflection was done. The time for action or death was upon him. And still the blood red gums, those hypnotically white teeth in jaggedly untidy rows, drew closer. The black eyes, almost as big as dinner plates at this point-blank range, disappeared beneath a milky white sheath, and he knew that this instinctive closure of the lids signalled the actual moment of attack. The instant of death.

The shark's speed increased dramatically and horrifyingly, and it leapt bodily out of the wave, straight at him, eyes still covered and acting on millions of years of blood-soaked instinct. Grayton threw himself down to lie on the board and clutch the rails in a vice-like embrace. A death grip. Time stopped, but, incredibly, the shark kept going. Its entire body sailed straight over him at waist height, clearing his prone body by about half a metre. As it flew over him, Grayton heard the mighty jaws snap shut with a hideous crunch, and then the beast splashed down in the white water to his left, missing his leg and board by millimetres. And Grayton kept surging forward with the broken wave.

The shark was behind him now, somewhere in the roiling foam, and he prayed it would take a few seconds for the thing to re-orient itself. He angled the board in towards the shallow rocky shore, hoping for once to hear and feel the dull thud and scrape of board on rock.

His mind screamed fear and anticipation, and at every moment he expected those monstrous jaws to crush his legs and mercilessly drag him back into deeper water. So he kicked and paddled furiously, and in less than four frightening seconds filled with a maddening mix of hope and despair, he reached the shallows.

He was being washed across the spiky rocks in less than a foot of water. But it was till too deep for Grayton, as images of white pointers beaching themselves to claim seals intruded on his fragile psyche. He slipped off his board and scrambled, slipped and flew across the biting limestone, oblivious to the barnacle cuts and lost toenail suffered in the process.

And then he was on dry land, ten metres from the water's edge, heaving with exertion and terror. There was no sign of the animal. It had simply disappeared, perhaps trying to tempt him back into the water with its absence. A temptation all too easily defeated. He took a few minutes to gather his breath, his wits and his strength, grabbed his mangled board, and started walking up the hill to the car park, trailing blood.

By the time he got to the car he'd moved past fear and become engulfed in an elated sense of gratitude that he was still alive and relatively intact. Getting dressed, he found himself giggling at the sheer magnitude of the event and the dimension of the terror he'd lived through. And by the time he drove into his carport, he was composing the statement he'd make to his mates over a beer that night: "Yeah, I saw the Drop In today at Dread Cove. Dropped in on me and tried to eat me. I said no way mate, my wave."

My Third Ear
(A true story)

By the seventh day of a Mentawai Islands trip, life looks pretty rosy. The initial froth has worn off, and the routine of surfing, sleeping, eating, and downing Bintangs, is well established.

We've been lucky so far this trip. The waves have been good to very good, not huge but more than generous in size and power. On the first morning here, I achieved my modest aim of riding into and spitting out of a good-sized E-Bay barrel, and every day since has been beautiful. We've enjoyed a medley of swells and directions, including several fortunate hours trading waves with just our crew at certain spots, and spent fun, funny nights in the big room at Pitstop Hill, reliving it all. We've surfed like frothing groms, dined like kings, drunk like fish, laughed like hyenas and slept like babies, and it's all been good.

This morning, the Pitstops reef at the base of our tsunami-proof hill was showing thick lines of clean energy, there was no more than a breath of wind, and the mood was high.

Before the sun was fully up I was paddling down to E-Bay looking to snag a solo slot or two, marvelling at this enchanted landscape and its magical ocean. The pyramidal hill that presides over Emerald Bay rose cool and dark on my right, and the swell shimmied in silently on my left.

There was a bit of 'morning sickness' about, a little rain-bearing front brought large, sloppy drops of rain, and a light northeasterly sprang up to ruffle the waters.

Because the tide was at its highest for the month, the lineup was a soup of debris. Coconuts and empty half-shells, branches, berries, sticks, leaves, fronds, husks, innumerable bits of unidentified detritus; anything that had found its way to the high tide mark in the last week or so was now bobbing around.

But the cool rain was welcome, the scenery mesmerising, and the intermittent sets comely. An occasional flash of lightning followed by the extended rumbling of distant thunder added to the air of mystery and expectation.

The first couple didn't quite live up to the promise – big sections dropped in front of me, barrels clamped shut, and once or twice the peak over-jacked so that a bungee jump was the only way in or out.

A couple of mates, Buzz and Steph, joined me, and we sat and yakked, debating where to sit, how to approach the wave, last night's slide show – the usual.

I'd pulled into a couple but not made any, and I was keen to get a good one under my belt. The morning sickness would probably settle and it would improve, but the crowd could fill in or, given recent volatile conditions, the wind might swing to almost any point on the compass at any moment.

Meanwhile, the Pitstop Hill boat, carrying a bunch of our crew around to the Playgrounds, had deviated to E-Bay to drop off Marc, the photographer. The prospect of nailing a couple of good water shots was energising.

Before Marc was even off the boat, which was now a hundred metres or so off the lineup, I had stroked into a likely-looking lump, almost immediately pulling into a gaping pit. It was never going to hold open, but I was hoping to get at least a half second "the view" before getting mashed. Then it seemed like the lip bit into my head with the speed and ferocity of a guillotine. It was a heavy crack, and it threw me off the board into the consuming foam. *Fuck*, I thought. *That lip is vicious.*

When I came up, I saw a squared length of milled hard-wood, probably a metre long and about 20 millimetres a side – maybe a cross-bar for a window pane – floating innocently next to me. I began to suspect that more than just water had been involved in smacking me down.

There was no time to think about it, though, because the next wave was rearing up, with a couple more behind it. Duck-diving that first one, the pain on the right side of my head intensified, and suspicions about the role of that piece of tim-ber deepened. I got through the set and put my hand to my head to see if there was blood, and poked two fingers into a deep, mushy hole. Steph saw me – the blood was starting to flow quite freely by that stage – and immediately started shouting and waving at the boat, which was about to move away. Buzz joined in, and I started paddling toward the boat, blood clouding the water with every stroke.

They waited until I got there, and as I climbed onto the boat, the look of concern on my mates' faces told a story.

'Jesus mate,' said Marty. 'You look like you've got a third ear.' He gave me his rash vest and I pressed it into the wound to stem the blood flow, and we headed back to camp. At the beach, Spanky took a couple of shots, and I could see what Marty had meant. The length of timber had opened up and pushed back a nice, fatty little flap of scalp, and it was sitting proud of my flattened hair.

Jake, a Pitstop Hill surf guide, came up the stairs with me, and Benny, a local boatman, carried my board. Paul Clark, the big cheese at Pitstop Hill, had a look and suggested it could be taken care of at Peipei, a village less than twenty minutes away on Siberut.

After a quick rinse and change into dry clothes, with a fresh dressing held to the now throbbing wound, I held up proceedings long enough to have a cup of tea and call my wife. Let's just say she was less than impressed. Then Paul, Rhys – a Pitstop Hill team member – and I jumped into a boat, and skipper An Simaepa piloted us across to Peipei.

There, we borrowed scooters, and Paul drove me up to the local medical centre. There was a power outage affecting the village – a regular event the Mentawai people take in their stride – but the friendly, cheerful and attentive staff directed me to a surgical bed by a window and got to work.

With no less than five nurses and a lady doctor crowding around me, working and watching, they cut away a pile of hair, very gently shaved and cleaned the wound area, and stitched it up. As they worked, the ladies chatted and gossiped and laughed, and if it hadn't been for the odd stabbing pain as needle pierced skin, it felt like I could have been on the beach in Bali having a massage. The only thing missing was someone trying to sell me a watch.

The medical centre staff were fantastic, and in short order I was released with eleven stitches in my melon, a handful of antibiotics and painkillers, and a bill for 150,000 rupiah – a princely fifteen dollars!

So now I'll sit it out for a few days lazing around like an old dog, maybe consume a few extra Bintangs, and listen to my mates recount their day's waves. Still, I count myself lucky to have walked away with such a clean, easily handled wound. There are a lot of ways E-Bay can hurt you, and although I hadn't quite thought of that one, it's definitely not the worst.

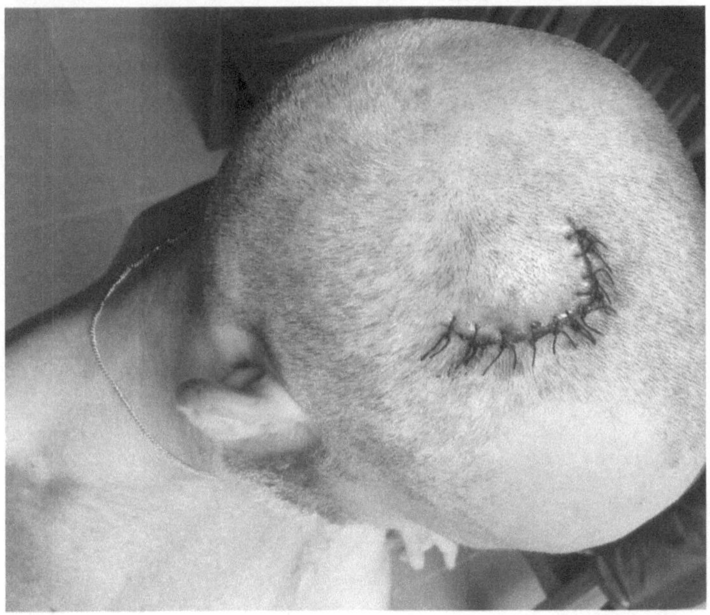

The end result (after a timely head shave from Marc). Terrific job by the team at Peipei Medical Centre.

Deepest thanks to Paul and Megan and the Pitstop Hill crew for the care and consideration they showed me during my funny little ordeal.

And apologies to my wife Rachel for sending through the gruesome pictures that so thoroughly alarmed her. That's apparently one hell of a way to break up a meeting.

Monday 14 May 2018
Pitstop Hill, Pulau Nyang Nyang
Kepulauan Mentawai
Sumatra Barat, Indonesia

Postscript — my mates scored excellent, epic and fun waves for the remainder of the week, and it was great to see how thoroughly they enjoyed themselves, but still tried to talk it down for my sake. Thanks for everything Steph, Buzz, Marty, Spanky, Worm, Trav, Shane, Iain and Redder, you blokes rock.

The Board

When they were nine years old, my little brother Jaxon and his best mate Tonk decided that the cool thing to do would be to take up surfing. So for weeks and weeks, Jaxon hassled my olds – and Tonk hassled his – until they were given surfboards. That was in 1983, and the board that my folks bought the kid was 5'10" and about 20" wide, almost three inches thick in the middle, and not much thinner at either end. Tonk's board was even worse – a single fin 6'0", intensely thick, flat and heavy. But as soon as they got their boards, the boys were right into learning to surf, and as the older, more experienced surfer (at 14, I'd been surfing for almost four years), it was up to me to teach them.

Day one in the surf couldn't have been tougher. There was a stiff onshore blowing, and the lumpy swell was running between four and six foot. "Forget it boys," I said to them. "If you go out there you'll drown! Wait here while I go for a surf." They protested, but I trotted out the old "I'll tell Mum and she'll take your boards away," threat, and they shut up and watched, pissed off, as I put on my wettie.

I paddled out through the hellish beach break, struggled through a set that arrived just in time to land on my head, and finally reached the peak. There were about five of us in the water, and we spent the next half hour being tossed around like undies in a washing machine, wind and spray in our eyes, salt in our throats, getting fuck all waves of any note for our trouble.

Meanwhile, on shore, Tonk and Jaxon had been getting more and more antsy, and eventually Tonk said, "Fuck this, I'm going out there." Of course, Jaxon had no option – if his mate was going out, so was he. Twenty minutes later, I was trying to find the rapidly shifting peak when Tonk appeared at my elbow. "Jesus Christ," I exploded, "what the fuck are you doing here?"

Tonk, tough little bastard that he was, looked me in the eye and said, "Well if you're allowed out here, I don't see why we can't come out."

"We?" I screamed. "You mean Jaxon's on his way out here? You little motherfuckers! You'll die!"

Tonk just looked at me with far too much cool for a nine year old, too stupid to be scared. A few minutes later, Jaxon appeared, breathless, wide-eyed with fear and beaming with pride at having made it out the back. I told the boys that unless they caught the first wave in and stayed onshore, I'd make sure they never set foot in the ocean with a surfboard ever again. They were shitting themselves by then anyway – having made it out to the peak they had no idea what to do next, and were clearly shocked by the amount of water moving around and the size of the waves. They agreed to take the next small one in.

Huey was having none of that though. Looking to the murky, cloudy horizon and an ocean whipped into a white-capped frenzy, we saw a huge sneaker set steam-rolling towards us. "Paddle!" I yelled at the boys, and started doing so myself, with all the speed I could muster. The wave started to crumble, then broke like a storm just in front of me. I duck dived as deeply as I could but was caught and rolled by the bastard.

By the time I came up, I was way out of breath, and there was another, even bigger wave behind. Again I took a sick pounding and came up gasping. There were no more sneakers behind that one, thank Christ.

I looked shorewards to see where Jaxon and Tonk had been, but all I could see was white water. Then I saw Tonk's board tomb-stoning in the middle of the impact zone, and the two halves of Jaxon's board floating not far away. Neither of the boys was visible, and I started to panic. I considered paddling into the impact zone, but figured that until I spotted the kids, I couldn't do anything in there except get the shit beaten out of me, so I waited a second.

At last, Tonk's head popped up, then Jaxon's, only a few metres from where the tail end of his board lay. His legrope had stood up to the pressure, so at least he had something to float with as he tried to make his way in.

A wave came, and I paddled for it, riding it all the way to shore on my belly. Then I turned back around and paddled out to meet the kids. They were swimming, crying and copping a bucketing from the pounding conditions, but they were alive. And after ten minutes of exhausting swimming and paddling with them I got the two of them onshore.

I've never seen an event that could bond two mates like that, before or since. Having almost drowned together, Tonk and Jaxon became even more and more like each other, and each was never far from the other. Almost every night of the week Tonk stayed over at our place or Jaxon camped over at his place, and they went everywhere together.

To my surprise, they went back into the water as soon as my old man bought Jaxon another board (we told him it'd been broken by some 'bullies' on the beach – if he knew the truth none of us would have ever surfed again).

The 'everywhere' that the boys went together was usually the beach, and they quickly became good, then excellent surfers. As grommets do, they joined the local boardriders club, but they never competed with each other, only surfing against others. It got so bad that if they were put in a heat together, they both forfeited: they'd both rather lose than subject the other to the humiliation of defeat. I used to tease them about being gay, but in truth they were just the best friends I've ever seen. And when they both started pulling the hottest chicks on the beach, I had to give away the 'homo' taunts.

As soon as they finished year twelve, Jax and Tonk got a flat together by the beach, which inevitably became the party house for a massive crew of locals. They were the cool kids we all wanted to be, and they were, of course, ultra-cool with it. As the older brother, I dropped in occasionally to wrench a couple with them or watch a surf vid, and many a Friday night my mates and I went to piss-ups in Crashland, as they called their place.

But then came the board. A six foot, four inch piece of polyurethane foam and fibreglass that achieved what no living creature had even attempted – it drove my brother Jaxon away from his best mate Tonk, and sowed the seeds of tragedy.

It appeared one day, hanging over the bar of our local pub, a garish beer logo plastered all over the deck; a sleek, razor thin, superfast babe of a board that, if it went as good as it looked, would instantly turn the rider into the next Kelly Slater. I was with the boys on a Friday afternoon when we first laid eyes on the glittering prize. To win it, all you had to do was drink the right brand of beer, and be there for the draw. The second they saw it, Tonk and Jaxon turned to each other and said in unison, "I'm gonna win that board."

The look of shock on their faces as they heard each other say it was hilarious – they were both startled to hear that the other was certain he was going to win the board, and both turned bright red with embarrassment. But instead of saying, "Ah sorry mate, I didn't know you wanted it…" as they normally would have done, Tonk turned to Jaxon and said, "You can't win it, I'm gonna."

This was a first. I'd never heard either of them challenge the other in anything – not since they almost drowned together, anyway. But Jaxon stood firm too. "Sorry mate, she's mine," he said. Suddenly there was a tension in the air. I decided to defuse the situation.

I looked at the two of them and said, "Sorry boys, that board is *mine*." I turned to the bar and ordered three of the requisite brand of beers. We stood at the bar for about half an hour, staring longingly at the board and talking about how much we'd shred on it after we won it. The moment of antagonism over the board passed quickly, and soon we were all pissed and doing our best to score with the chicks that were rocking in.

The draw for the board raffle was scheduled for 10.00pm the following Friday, and by 9.30 the crowd was amped. But none more so than my brother Jaxon. He'd spent the week drinking that foul beer and staring at the board, and by that stage he was fully convinced that he was going to win it. And I have to admit that when I heard Jaxon telling people, "I'm gonna win a board on Friday night," as though he were stating a well known fact, I got a weird feeling he was right. He was gonna win.

Of course, almost everyone in the pub was saying, "I'm gonna win that board," but most were saying it in hope; Jaxon said it from conviction.

And then a funny thing happened.

Tonk came up while I was talking to Jaxon and said, "Mate, I tell you what. If I win that board, I'll give it to you!"

We looked at Tonk, and once again I thought to myself, "Christ, these guys'll do anything for each other."

But Jaxon looked hard into the eyes of his best friend, and there was none of the gratitude and mateship that I expected. There was only a look of what I would call surprised disgust.

"You fucking arsehole!" he said, to the shock and horror of both Tonk and myself. I looked at Jaxon to make sure I'd heard right, and he repeated it.

"You fucking, fucking, fucking arsehole. You know as well as I do that I'm going to win that board, and you're using our friendship to try and score it. You want me to say 'ah shit mate, and if I win, I'll give it to you'. Well I ain't gonna do that – I'm gonna win it and keep it. I'll let you ride it any time you like, but *that*," and he pointed at the board hanging over their heads, "is my board. And I tell you mate, I never expected you to try a trick like that on me."

Tonk protested, but Jaxon had obviously hit the nail on the head. He'd picked up Jaxon's ultra-positive vibe and he knew as well as I did that if any of us was going to win that board, it was going to be Jaxon.

And while I was disappointed in Tonk for Jaxon's sake, I wasn't all that surprised. He'd always had an eye for the main chance, and had never been above a bit of trickery to get what he wanted. It was just that he'd never used it against his best mate before.

Thirty minutes later, Jaxon was triumphantly holding the board aloft, screaming, "I fuckin' told ya!" to Tonk over the noise of the crowd.

Both of the boys were beaming, and there was no hint of the spat Tonk had provoked with his dubious offer, so I assumed that was the end of it. We took turns carrying the board back to Crashland after the pub closed, staggering pissed and singing victory songs in Swahili.

When we got there we arced up a late night choof and carefully put the board on the table. It was the only time that table every got fully cleaned.

We examined every millimetre, touched every curve, and fingered every rail over and over again. We held it up to the light and marvelled at how sharply and severely the nose was pointed, we looked along the bottom to suss the depth and width of the concave and the way it transitioned from a double to a single so smoothly. We inspected the stringer and caressed the deck, and then did it all again and again.

At about 2.30am, I staggered out of there, leaving Tonk and Jaxon sat staring glazy-eyed at the board, mumbling drool-soaked utterances to each other.

When Jaxon took the board out next morning, from the first wave he ripped. It was about five foot at our local reef break, fairly solid and tubing top to bottom. Jaxon and Tonk were out there at dawn, practically sitting on top of each other in the lineup as usual. But when I paddled out about an hour after sunrise, I could see that there was a bit of strain between the boys. They argued as they sat waiting for a set wave.

"Man, you said I could ride it!" said Tonk. Jaxon stonewalled him, shaking his head. "Yeah, and I will," he replied, "but this is the first time I've ever ridden it, and I'm carving like I've never done before! Let me have at least this one surf for myself!"

"But I was going to give you that board!" Tonk protested. Jaxon reacted violently, pushing his mate in the chest.

"You tried to trick me out of this board Tonk, and I won't forget that, and I won't fuckingwell forgive it either. Now if you won't let me surf in peace, I'll take me fuckin' board and go home!"

"Ah fuck ya, I've had enough of this anyway!" said Tonk. "You and your precious board can stay out here, and I hope you fuckin' drown!" he called as he paddled away.

"Don't ding your board on the rocks mate – it's the only one you've got!" called Jaxon as his best mate caught a wave and headed shorewards. I looked at my brother and said, "Mate, I've never seen you act like that with Tonk…"

Jaxon looked me square in the eye and said, "He never made a complete cunt of himself like that before…or maybe I just never noticed."

He only surfed for another ten minutes or so. The poor bastard's day had obviously been ruined by the argument. He paddled in looking gloomy, and left me to the crumbling, on-shore conditions that had crept in. It was a bummer seeing my brother so aggro like that, but I figured that Tonk had been taking him for a bit of a ride for a few years – you know, pinching a bud here or borrowing ten bucks there and never intending to pay it back. So maybe it was time they had it out. I wasn't wrong.

That afternoon, the boys had an almighty blue. From what the neighbours told me, it was pretty full on, and the sounds blasting out of the flat included breaking glass, the grunting and thumping of a wrestling match, and a stream of vicious and cruel profanities that lit up the entire street. By that night, when I dropped in for a beer, the fight was over and the boys were sitting watching a surf video, occasionally talking to each other in monosyllables.

Next morning, I woke up on the couch at Crashland to find Jaxon storming about the place with a desperate look on his face. Tonk had gone, and he'd taken Jaxon's new board with him. My brother was howling mad, and nothing I could do would calm him.

He grabbed Tonk's board and sprinted over to the beach with me not far behind. He paddled out as fast as he could, and long before he got to the break, he was screaming at Tonk, who just laughed. Reaching Tonk, Jaxon had grabbed the nose of his board and really paid out on him, and Tonk retaliated in kind. At last, Jaxon said, "Get off my board right now mate, or I swear I'll kill you!"

Tonk, who was sitting about two metres away by this stage, leaned back on Jaxon's board, dug the tail deep in the water and slipped off with a vicious sneer written on his face. The board shot forward, took a neat half-spin, and the nose speared Jaxon straight through the trachea. The water surged in through the gaping hole as he struggled to stay afloat, and blood and screams mingled in the water.

I got to him as fast as I could, but it was too late. I cradled his head as my little brother died an agonising, terrified death there on the water, his last breath bubbling out a curse on his best mate's life.

We buried the board with Jaxon. Tonk hanged himself in jail while on remand for manslaughter, unable to cope with the magnitude of what he'd done. He'd let a piece of fibreglass and foam come between him and the best friend he would ever have. Let it destroy the only real thing in his life.

It took me years to get over it, and even now I can feel the emotion welling up as I write. And any time I walk into a pub and see a surfboard hanging over the bar with a sign saying, "Win this board!" I walk straight out again.

Belief

There are days on surf trips when no surfing gets done. The swell disappears or the onshore comes up or, as in the case of the trip I'm thinking of, both.

We were huddled around in our big 'kitchen' tent several hundred kilometres from the nearest town, hiding from the vicious westerly that was whipping squalls of red dust and debris around the camp, occasionally hurling unknown heavy objects against the tent's thin fabric sides. It was a long, boring, shitty day, and we didn't even have enough booze to while it away getting faceless. So we sat and talked bullshit.

Stories about heinous surf trips and epic waves, evil ex-girl-friends, magic boards and wicked cars, hectic fights, fabulous fucks, narrow escapes and tragedies – just about everything got an airing. The master storyteller of the group was Victor. He was the oldest, the gnarliest, and by a fairly long margin the ugliest of us, but he was also the smartest and the wisest – because those two things are not the same. When he spoke, we listened.

So when old Vic noisily cleared his throat as Glassy wound down his well-worn story about that one time he shared a barrel with Made Something-or-other at Padang-Padang (with Glassy the deeper of the two of course) we were all ears.

"Belief," said Vic with that self-satisfied smile he gets when he's already decided on every word of the whole story, and he knows the crew will be spellbound.

"I tell ya, this shit is all about belief, boys. Not the kind of belief you might need to suspend when you listen to Glassy spin his fuckin' fairy-tale about ridin' the foamball in Padang fuckin' Padang. I'm talking about self-belief. It can make the difference between making it or not making it, winning or losing, and sometimes even life or death. Now don't get too excited, the yarn I'm about to tell ya isn't one of those life or death things, but it does show ya how far a little belief can go.

"Years ago, when you blokes were all still shittin' in Huggies and your idea of a good dinner was a can of stewed apples, there was a bloke we called Tony Danza. His real name was Daniel or something, but we called him Tony Danza because he had a big pile of black hair and an even bigger nose, and because he was forever asking, 'who's in charge here?' And if you don't know who Tony Danza is or why we'd call him that, then you're too fuckin' young to know shit, but he was on a show called 'Who's the Boss'. Get it?

"And if ya don't, even meatheads like you should be able to figure out that calling this bloke Tony Danza was something of a compliment. Now, Tony wasn't a bad surfer, but he wasn't great, you know. He made his own boards, too, and this is where it gets a bit weird. Cos although they looked like crap, he did a pretty good job of 'em. Well we guessed he did, because once he started riding his own boards, he started to do better in the local comps. Never won, but never came dead last either – not by a long shot. Thing is, when he made boards for any of the other blokes, nobody ever rode 'em more than a few times. They were shit.

"He'd make a board for some punter and give it to him, and a week later the punter'd come back and go, 'Tony, this thing is a fuckin' dog.' And Tony'd take it out and tear the bag out of every wave he attacked on it, just carve the fucker up. It seemed that it wasn't the board, it was just that Tony only knew how to make the things for himself. He had an instinct about where to put the foam, how hard to make the rails, and how much rocker and concave and all that fuckin' shit, for himself. And if nobody else could ride it, well they could go and fuck 'emselves.

"But still, he never got closer to winning the local comp than the quarters. Just couldn't do it. 'It's the fins,' he'd say. 'The fuckin' fins.' He never could find a set of fins he thought would give him the edge. So he went, 'right, I'll make me own fuckin' fins,' and that's what he did.

"He studied tuna fins, marlin fins, dol-phins (ha ha) bar-racuda fins, garfish fins, pike fins, shark fins, whale fins, the fins on rockets – every fuckin' fin he could find. Then he went off and he studied aerodynamics, hydrodynamics, thermo-fuckin'-dynamics, quantum mechanics and christ knows what-all, and he went to work.

He made the nastiest, strangest, shittest looking fins you ever saw. I mean, they were like blowie fins, but less classy. They were blocky, angular, bloated and just plain repulsive. But fuck me, they worked! Old Tony started winning club comps. With that shithouse looking board of his, and those fuckin' atrocious fins, he was rippin'. Couldn't put a foot wrong, and didn't give a bugger what the conditions were – big, small, onshore, offshore, fat, hollow, whatever. For about three years he couldn't be beaten, strolling away with the club championship like he was born to it.

"Then at the height of his reign, he retired. Bang. Just like that, gave it away. He donated his magic board and those hideous fuckin' fins to the club, and every club champ for the last twenty years has tried to ride 'em without a smidgeon of success. They're fuckin' shit. I can tell ya straight that it's true, because I've tried to ride 'em myself, and I ain't exactly a slouch." This was true, Vic was an epic surfer.

"You know what propelled Tony Danza to glory? It sure as shit wasn't his equipment, so it could only be one thing: belief. The trouble with old Tony is, he put all his belief into his boards and his fins, and that's what carried him along. He shoulda just believed in himself. And let that be a lesson to ya."

Outside, the wind screamed, the flying spinifex beat against the tent walls, and the ocean kept up its impression of a washing machine. And I don't know why, but suddenly I was dead keen to go surfing.

The Seed

Some blokes are born to surf, and Jack Baird was one of them. He revelled in the big stuff, no matter how big. No matter how ugly the drop, how dry the shelf, how heavy the lip or how harsh the beating he knew he'd receive, Baird would take it on.

So on this one day, when it was a rare eight to ten with rogue twelve foot sets at his home break, he didn't give a stuff that it was hideously onshore, he was out there, making a few and taking a few awful canings, having a ball.

As usual when it was like that, he was on his own, but that was the way Baird liked it. Too hard for any other bastard was still not hard enough for him. He was surprised, then, to see a weedy little bloke turn up out the back between heaving sets, but in his typically friendly way he grinned and said g'day.

Jack Baird knew and was known by everybody in those parts, but this bloke was a complete stranger. Now, he wasn't going to hold that against the only other punter brave or stupid enough to paddle out on such a gnarly day, so he yakked to him a bit about the drop, the shape, the breeze. The bloke didn't really say much, just nodded and said yeah in the manner of a man who doesn't make friends easily. The fear in his eyes was enough for Jack to know that just being out there was enough of an effort for the poor bastard, so he left him alone. Jack's surprise at the mysterious stranger's presence out there grew – along with his admiration – when a fourteen foot bomb speared out of the murk, and the little bastard paddled into it.

Man and board disappeared over the edge of a fast moving mountain of water, and gently cursing the bloke for taking probably the wave of the day, Baird turned to wait for the next macker. Only a couple of seconds later, though, he heard a faint howl over the thunder of the breaking waves and the screech of wind and spray. He spun around and scanned the paddock-sized impact zone to see the stranger floating fair in the middle of it – boardless and about to take an eight footer directly on the head.

The bugger was in trouble, and Baird did what he had to do. He stroked into a completely unmakeable screamer, took a death drop into hell and copped a savage thrashing. By the time he surfaced his legrope had snapped and he was boardless too, but he was pretty close to the seriously struggling, scared witless stranger. He grabbed him and started swimming to shore.

Twenty-five exhausting minutes, a series of poundings, and a strength-sapping swim of epic proportions later, with him doing all the work, Baird and the stranger lay on the beach together, knackered. Jack recovered first, got up and walked along the beach to grab his board and the two halves of the stranger's board, and hauled the whole lot, including the stranger himself, to the carpark. He saw the guy safely to his car, then went to his own wagon to get changed. While he was drying off, the still pale stranger came over to thank Baird for saving his life.

"Eh, no worries mate!" said Jack with a grin. "Surfing with dead guys kinda sucks anyway, ay?"

The stranger smiled thinly and held out his open palm. In it there was a single, tiny seed. Shiny black, and almost round, but a little almond shaped too.

"My friend, I'd like to give you something for saving me. Something very special. Plant this seed, and nurture well the plant that it becomes. The seeds that it will produce are unique, of fabled power. When you plant them, no new shrub, no new bush will grow, for this is the last fertile seed of its kind. But the seeds that you harvest from this last plant will summon swell. Plant one seed, and even on the flattest midsummer's day, it will call a solid swell from the depths."

Baird didn't want to offend the guy, and took the seed as humbly as he could, while trying to stifle his laughter.

"I can see you don't believe me my friend," said the stranger. "But that is no matter. In a day or so this swell will be gone. Plant this seed when it is flat, and the next day enjoy the best surf of your life. I guarantee it.

"When you see the power of this swell summoning seed, you will be more than eager to care for the plant – the very last of its kind." Baird pocketed the black seed, thinking it couldn't hurt to try.

A week or so later, it had been flat for several days, and prospects for a swell looked bleak. The charts on the internet showed nothing for thousands of k's.

"Fuck it," said Baird to himself. "I'll bung it in the ground. Can't hurt." And he took the seed out to his back yard and carefully planted it in a good spot.

Next day he did his daily dawn run to the beach – and had to bolt home for a gun. Unbelievably, a macking ten foot swell, clean and hollow, had come out of nowhere and was assaulting the beach. Baird took it on in his usual hellman style, and had probably the surf of his life. The swell lines were so straight, the banks so shallow and the waves so incredibly perfect, it was just not possible. And the whole time he was out there, Jack Baird was thinking to himself, "Jesus, it works! It fuckin' works! I'm gonna have a plant that produces seeds that summon the swell. Holy hell!"

The next ten weeks were the longest of his life. A couple of days after the short-lived miracle that the locals dubbed 'The Impossible Swell' died, a little green bud poked its head out of the ground where Baird had buried the seed. He was overjoyed. And as the flat weeks of summer eked by, he carefully tended and nurtured the little plant, watching it grow. He told no one, even though his mates were constantly parading through his house, and he was dying to spill the beans about it.

Finally, after weeks and weeks of tense anticipation, wondering whether he'd overwatered or underwatered, hoping it wasn't getting too much sun or too little, a handful of seeds appeared in a weird flower-like bud on the plant. Ten days later, one of them had gone black, and it was time. As usual, there hadn't been much more than a dribble for weeks, so Jack was ready for the big trial. Next day was forecast for an all day onshore though, so he bided his time until the following evening, when the next day's forecast was for a light offshore.

He carefully removed the black seed from the plant, and as the sun set, planted it in the yard.

Next morning he was up before dawn, and down at the beach with his big board on the roof of his car. And he wasn't disappointed. It was huge, and he was the only one who was prepared for it. While the other earlies were heading back home for bigger boards, Jack scored the biggest, heaviest, longest stand-up barrel of his entire surfing career. The surf was totally maxing, and Baird was a grinning, frothing fool.

While everyone else sat there and said, "Fuck! Where did this swell come from?" Baird congratulated himself, and thought, "I'll never have to live through a flat spell again." But then it occurred to him that he only had the one plant, and that it would have a limited supply of seeds. If only he could grow more plants like that…

Paddling out after an all time cavern on a thick ten-footer, he had a brainstorm.

"Holy shit! I can get Conan the Ganja Barbarian to clone the plant. He knows all that hydroponics stuff, it'll be a piece of piss for him. I can have a garden full of swell summoning plants. I'll definitely never have to live through another flat spell ever again!"

For the whole rest of the surf, Baird's head was swimming with plans and ideas. Where to put the clones, where to take his seeds once he had a good stock of them, how to take care of his garden, and how to keep Conan quiet about it. After an hour or so he couldn't take it – he wanted to start immediately. So he caught a wave in and headed home.

Pulling up outside his place, he was pleased to see that he wouldn't have to call Conan, because his car was outside Jack's place, which meant that the man himself must be inside. As usual the bastard had let himself in. Baird walked into the lounge room, and there, as usual, was Conan in a haze of blue smoke. In front of him there was a pile of freshly clipped, microwave dried green leaves – all the same colour as Jack's swell-summoning plant.

"Man, I've never seen a mull plant like that before," said Conan. "But I gotta tell ya, that is good shit. Too bad it was going to seed, eh? I probably did ya a favour by ripping it out."

When, not where.

Owl Thomas used to live across the road from me. A totally committed surfer, Owl was a big, grizzly sort of a bloke with a fully charged gleam in his eyes and a ferocious approach to everything. But he wasn't your average surf bum; he had a stack of degrees that would make a grown professor tremble: he was a physicist, engineer, chemist and philosopher all in one unkempt package.

I used to hang out over at Owl's house, hoping that some of his cool would rub off on me, watching while he got up to all sorts of weird stuff. He designed wild looking surfboards with triangular fins and channels across the bottom instead of along it, he made his own solar oven, which he fed with power at night from solar batteries of his own design, and his house was filled with handy little knick-knacks that he'd knocked up. He once even showed me a sketch for a wave-generating machine he'd designed that produced ten foot plus waves.

He was inventive, eccentric, and a genuine legend on our local beach. Whenever the winter swells started jacking, he was the first out there, taking off deeper and steeper than anyone else, and carving more radically than you'd think possible for such a big bastard. He was good at everything without being a prick about it. So, naturally, most people didn't bother to try to understand him, and the rest hated him!

But then, the Owl started to go a little funny. Okay, *funnier*. He stopped making dinky little, fancy looking machines and gadgets, and began spending an intense amount of time with his head down, reading massive, heavy looking books, and scribbling indecipherable equations in a thick, dog-eared notebook. I'd go over there and he'd only stop long enough to mutter something like, "multiply Planck's constant by the precise volume of matter to be transported, double the rate of expansion in the particle acceleration chamber and realign the plasma field…"

"What are you doing?" I'd say.

But he'd only laugh and say, "you'll learn in time. In time." And then let out a huge cackle, as though he found those two words incredibly funny.

Then he started building this huge thing in the backyard. Perfectly circular, with a domed aluminium roof, inside it had a thick, round, strange looking column covered with lights, digital readouts and buttons in the centre of it. The sloping walls were covered with what looked like beaten copper, and all around the inside he'd installed rows of empty racks and cupboards, and not much else.

He laboured over that thing for months, stopping for a few days here and there to delve back into the books or go online, then beginning the building frenzy anew, re-wiring what he called "the drive column", sticking strange antennae on the roof, or mucking around in the electronic bowels of the thing.

One day, I went over there to tell him that it was clean off-shore and four foot, and I thought he'd drop everything and go for his board, but he just kept tinkering with that bloody machine. I made the bastard stop what he was doing and look me in the eye.

"Come on, Owl," I said. "What's going on? You haven't surfed in over two months, and that's not just out of character, it's completely unbelievable."

He looked at me as though he was about to say something, then obviously changed his mind. His expression closed up a bit as he said, "It's the crowds, kid. I hate the crowds." He wasn't lying, but neither was he telling the whole truth.

"Bullshit!" I protested. "You're the most respected local on the whole coast! You get any wave you want, and no one would dare drop in on you. How could crowds affect you?"

"It's still crowded, kid. And dirty. I dream of a place where I can surf alone, unhassled by people, in clean, shitless water. A place where nobody surfs but me. Understand?"

"Yeah, I know what you mean," I said. "But there's no such place is there? Not on this planet, anyway."

"Ah. No. Not on this earth, not any more. But once…"

And that gleam shafted from his eyes, sharp and clear but distant. Then he kind of snapped back to attention, his head disappeared inside his books, and I obviously ceased to exist for him. I let myself out.

Several more weeks passed. They had to close down a section of our beach for a couple of weeks because of an oil spill. A war started somewhere in the Middle East. Disease, apathy and crime ran riot around the world, as they have done for the whole of my life. I mentioned these things to Owl, but rather than fly into his usual rage over these disgraces, he merely shrugged his shoulders philosophically and said, "It's the times we live in, kid. The times we live in."

The next time I went into Owl's backyard contraption, because I couldn't find him in the house, the racks were crammed with surfboards. Heaps of them, like thirty or forty – everything from 5'8" fish to 10, 11 foot guns lined the walls. There were quite a few wetsuits, too – again, all types, from vests and short johns to steamers, plus boots, gloves and hoods. Unlike the surfboards, the wetsuits were all one size: Owl's. I was certain that he'd cracked.

"OK, this is getting beyond bizarre," I said. "What the fuck are you doing with all this stuff?"

"Well, seeing as how I'm pretty much done, I'll tell you kid. I'm leaving."

"I figured something like that was up. But where are you going, and how are you going to carry all that stuff?"

"I'd tell you where I'm going, if I could just figure out when! Now you'd better piss off, and let me get back to work."

A couple of days after that, as I was coming home from a late afternoon surf, Owl called me over and together we went into his machine.

"Kid," he said, "take a look. She's finished! Ain't she a beaut? I'm taking her out of here tonight." I nodded. The interior of the machine looked like a surfer's wet dream with all those boards and gear. I looked around in longing and admiration. But Owl kept talking.

"Actually, I don't know if I'm going anywhere, really. Tell you the truth, I'm a bit nervous, and I'd hate to just disappear without a trace, so I figure you're my link. If you get a message from me, you'll know I've succeeded. If not, you'll know I'm out there…somewhere." As he spoke, he waved his arms around dramatically.

"And how are you going to send me a message from 'out there'?" I asked, amused. I was used to his crackpot ways. But he was still serious.

"Kid, if I make it, I won't be 'out there', I'll be right here, just back then." Right. That made sense.

"You didn't get some of that brown acid off Davo, did you?" I asked. His huge face darkened to a scowl. "I'm dead set about this, and all I need is a little reassurance. But if you don't want to provide it, I'll go find some other smartarse kid…"

"OK, where will this message come from?" I asked in my gravest tone, asking myself if I should notify the authorities so they could come and pick him up and lock him in a loony bin.

"I'll bury it right outside my front door," he said, walking to the door of the contraption and tapping the dead grass there with his toe. "Come over tomorrow, bring your shovel, and dig right here."

"Great," I said. "And what am I supposed to find?"

He smiled.

"Don't you worry about that, you'll know it when you see it. Just come over tomorrow and dig, you hear?"

"I hear you, Owl." I wondered how much he'd hate me if I had him taken to the rubber room, but decided I'd see how he was the next day. Then he shook my hand, wished me a good life, and sent me away, reminding me yet again to dig in the agreed spot next day. I walked back over the road to my home convinced that poor old Owl was going nowhere but the funny farm.

Early the next morning, I was heading out to check the surf, and as I went past, I peered over the Owl's fence. The bloody monstrosity he'd built had gone. Vanished! The back-yard was empty.

"Bullshit!" I thought. "He must have needed a crane and a semi-trailer at least to get that thing out, but I didn't hear a thing last night. What's the bugger up to now?"

I looked through a window into his house – it still had most of the furniture there, and a few other bits and pieces, but it also had that unlived in, abandoned look about it. I couldn't believe that he'd really gone.

So I put my board down, darted home and got a shovel, and took it to the big dead patch in the middle of the backyard where the gizmo had been standing just the day before. At the spot where the door used to be, I started to dig – even though it was pretty obvious that nothing had been buried under the flattened grass there in the last twenty-four hours.

About two feet down, I found a stout metal box that looked old and weathered. I dug it out and opened it up. I still can't believe what I found. Maybe it was a joke. But it certainly looked authentic, and it looked as though it had been there for a long, long time.

There was an envelope addressed to Jimson Talbot & Co, Lawyers, a copy of the deeds to his house, and a second envelope, labelled *The Kid*. I figured that must be me, because there was no one else Owl called Kid. I opened it, and here's what it said:

Kid,

I made it! Believe it or not, I've gone back in time, and I'm sitting here at the end of the nineteenth century! And I love it! You see, a while ago I had this idea about matter transference through the space-time continuum via magnetic energy field reversal. I won't bore you with the details because even a smartarse kid like you would never understand it, but it bloodywell works! So here I am back here with all these people who've been dead for over a hundred years, if you know what I mean.

I haven't moved an inch in space, but what a difference the move in time has made. The spot where our houses stand – in your time – is still unexplored bush in my time, and it's still a two hundred metre walk through it to get to the beach. The fully deserted beach! I've been here about five weeks now, and I'm getting a handle on how to deal with the people of this century. Fuck, are they backward! It's great – no phones, cars, tv, radio, nothing. And best of all, not a soul in the surf. No one.

Of course, when the few people that get down to the beach here see me paddling out in what to them is fearsome surf, wearing my twentieth century wetsuit and riding my twentieth century board, they kind of freak out, but they're getting used to it. At first they thought I was some kind of sea monster (one asshole even shot at me!), but now they just leave me alone.

Kid, I wish you were here to share the waves with me (shit, I never thought I'd say that!), but I wasn't sure if this thing would work, and didn't want to risk your life along with mine. If I'd known it would be this good, I would have brought you for sure. I'll be buying a boat soon – straight after the Melbourne Cup. The Sports History book I brought with me tells me that Archer will win this year (thank you Back to the Future!*) and I'll be backing him with everything I've got. That ought to buy a pretty nice boat, eh?*

I could use a crewman. But it's a little late now. So as a consolation prize, the house is yours. I've left the title deeds in the box, and a letter for my lawyers. See them and they'll sort it out. Anyway, gotta go - it's four foot, offshore and screaming out to be ridden. Have a great life, and don't let the crowds get to ya!

Owl

Postscript.

When I put this weird tale down on paper a few years ago, I still only half believed it, and was more inclined to the view that Owl had done a runner for reasons of his own.

But now I'm convinced that it's true, not least because the lawyers came through and I own what used to be Owl's place. Even more convincing, recently I was looking through some old newspapers for a research project I'm involved in, and I came across this article from the Eastern Gazette of September 27, 1862.

Water Trickster Enthralls Beach Crowd

Visitors to Sydney's Bondi Beach were astounded and amazed at the antics of a water gymnast of extraordinary skill at the weekend. The man, clad in a sleek, skintight bathing costume and looking like something out of a novel by Mr HG Wells, had a short, pointed platform with which he "rode" the breakers as they rolled onto the beach.

Identified as Mr Brian Thomas, he defied the power of the waves, riding them with seeming ease and confidence, shooting great plumes of spray about as he executed one audacious manoeuvre after another. After over three hours practising his "surfing" as he calls it, Mr Thomas emerged from the water to promise a repeat performance, possibly as early as Monday morning, weather permitting, which promise drew a round of applause from the crowd.

So it's true. Time travel is real, and somewhere back in the nineteenth century Owl Thomas is sailing the world with a lifetime's worth of boards and wetsuits, and all the great waves of the world there for his use alone. The prick.

Lost and Found

"There's something about being driven," I said to myself. I was holding a brand new board, staring at perfect Hawaiian surf, unable to go surfing. I had a plane ticket in my hand and I knew I had to catch that plane. My business demanded it.

Standing there, watching the waves, feeling that special slick grace of new fibreglass under my arm, I tried to figure out just what it is about being driven. All I knew was that, from a young age, I'd pushed myself to perform beyond my potential. Willed myself to over-achieve in everything I attempted.

This, I believed, was a good thing. After all, it had brought me here, to the point of being the stupidly rich owner of a software company at 29. About to leave paradise.

When I'd told my only surfing mate that I was going to Hawaii, he'd immediately asked what boards I'd be taking. I told him that it was a business trip, not a holiday. He looked at me as if I'd just landed from Mars.

"Scotty, you can't go to Hawaii and not surf! You don't have to charge ten foot Pipe to have the surf of your life. My God! Hawaii. You *have* to surf," he said, almost pleading. I thought he was being a bit melodramatic.

For me, business and surfing had always been separate, and business had come first for quite a few years. Sure, I still went surfing, but it was always more of a mission than a pure pleasure trip. An excuse to consult weather charts for days in advance, to pore over predictions, read and reread surf reports, check wave buoys and surfcams, and devour a deluge of images and information around the destination and the trip. An opportunity to plan the packing and the travel, the arrival and departure times, the meals, the side trips, the pre- and post-surf activities. A mandate to create a meticulous itinerary, and to carry it off diligently.

The simple act of surfing itself meant a chance to undertake an endless array of internal assessments and evaluations. Every wave had to be dissected, examined move by move and turn by turn, over and over again. The conditions too played their part, and must be monitored and recorded for comparison to the predictions: the swell height, direction and speed, the breeze, the number of times surfed in that place and in what conditions, the crowd, the tide; factors I analysed, compartmentalised, rationalised and criticised, and stored away for future reference.

Even the quickest, as-near-to-spontaneous-as-I-could-be run to the local reef break was a project. A challenge to be surmounted. Another example of being driven.

I never mixed surfing with work — they each held separate goals and challenges, and when I did one, I focused on it completely and was blind to the other. Although I'd been overseas countless times in my work, not once had I ever even considered taking a board.

And here I was, standing, watching perfect Hawaiian surf, holding a new board. The limo driver was urging me to get into the car and go to the airport, or I might miss my plane. I got into the car, awkwardly shoving in the board on the seat opposite me. As the chauffeur drove to the airport I realised I'd never actually enjoyed anything for its own sake. Everything I'd ever done had been a task, a set of obstacles to overcome, a series of waypoints on the journey to success. Of course it was satisfying in a way. In many ways. But if I ever had it, I'd lost the art of experiencing something for the sheer joy of it all. Somehow, I'd forgotten how to completely relax.

The conference earlier that afternoon had finished two hours early – one of the speakers had failed to turn up. So I was out of there with three hours to spare, looking for a quest with which to fill the spare time. The thought had struck me, why not take a new board home?

My mates would be impressed, and I could easily fill in a couple of hours sorting through racks of boards, comparing rocker and bottom shape, tail types and plans, pondering fin options, considering length, width, volume, rail sharpness and deck roll. Hell, I could treat it as another statistical journey, arrive at the most logical purchase and buy it. It wouldn't be (it never was) an emotional decision.

I set upon the task eagerly, spending a full hour dissecting the merits of nearly every board in the first shop I went into, holding them all, feeling them, discussing the ins and outs of the design with the surprisingly knowledgeable assistant.

But the moment I walked into the second shop, my plans went awry. There on the rack, right in front of me, was The Board. A 6' 8" pintail, quite pronounced nose rocker and tail-lift, light single concave through to Vee bottom, hard rails, FCSII with a set of Swiss made H4 fins in quad configuration.

It was truly an insane shape, decorated with the most amazing spray job I'd ever seen. The whole board was a giant microchip, every gate and switch present in meticulous detail. A work of art as much as a surfboard, and so obviously mine. What better board for the CEO of a software company?

Walking out of the shop with my purchase, I was struck for the first time by the idea that I should surf it there and then. Get a bit of the Hawaiian juice for which it was made. For a moment I was simply stunned by the change that seemed to be overtaking me. Minutes after making probably the first emotionally led decision of my adult life, I was contemplating an impetuous action.

And then I realised it was too late to actually surf; I had to think seriously about getting to the airport. So I had the chauffeur drive by the beach, where I just held the board and watched. As I sat in the limo, speeding to the airport, I said to myself, "This board will change the way I look at surfing. And work. And life."

But work was busy when I got back. We had a new product going online, and even though the first release was simply a free Beta version, orders were pouring in for the release version. Surf trips were put on hold for a couple of weeks, and then a couple of months. Not only was I back to being driven, it was foot flat to the floor stuff.

One Sunday, months after I'd bought it, I finally took my

new board – which I'd inevitably christened The Microchip –
for a paddle. It was head high (big for our beach) mush, but
to my mind, and on that board, it was an incredible surf. The
'Chip surfed every bit as sharp as it looked, and for the whole
session I carved. Feeling proud of myself, I stopped in at the
local beer garden for a few ales with the locals on the way
home. When I came out an hour later, the board was gone
from the roof of my car.

I was pissed off. Angry at myself for leaving it on the roof
so carelessly. Furious with the thief for having the gall and the
bastardry to steal it. Livid that our world has degraded to such
a state, where people habitually and thoughtlessly treat each
other so badly.

And on the sombre drive home, I formulated a new mission.
The product launch had been a huge success, and now I had
the time and the energy to devote to the single-minded act of
finding my board. Whatever it took, I would find and retrieve
my board, and bring that prick to justice.

Inside of a couple of days, I had a link on practically every
commercial and private surfing related website in the world.
Any time a surfer logged on to a surfcam to see their local
conditions, scan a surf report, check the weather or get a buoy
reading, plan a trip, check competition results, chat to other
surfers or simply stare at surf pictures, they saw a picture of
my board and an offer of a substantial reward. It was a unique,
easily identifiable board, and I was supremely confident that I
would get a result.

After two weeks of absolutely no response, I wasn't so sure.
Then, as I was about to turn my full attention back to work
and write the whole experience off, an email came through.

From Augusta, Western Australia. It said:

"G'day Mate,

I was up at Gracetown the other day and saw a bloke on a board like this. Was pretty solid 8' – 10' at North Point and this guy was ripping it to bits. Just dropping in to the nastiest pits and shralping it like he owned the place. Geezuss that board goes! And the bloke riding it's got nurries of steel. I spoke to him for a good long while in the lineup – top bloke, too. I reckon if that's your board, he's not the bloke that stole it: he's far too cool to be a bandit. Anyway, he said he'll only be around for a bit because he's got a job to do, so I thought I'd let you know.

Personally I reckon he must have a board like yours, but I thought you'd like to know.

Cheers,

Boonie."

There was no other board like mine, of that I was sure. Thirty-six hours later I was in Augusta, on Boonie's doorstep. We had a long conversation, and he told me about the thief, and the surf they'd shared together.

It sounded like surf to die for – big, perfect and glassy, with loads of power through every section. It sounded, too, like he had definitely seen my board – a razor-sharp pin, crazy speed down the line but super-responsive, with an awesome ability to snap chunks off a wave. I'd seen the potential for these things in my board, but of course I'd never experienced them. Because that bastard had stolen it before I ever could. I was hotter than ever for him, and more determined than ever to get my board back.

Boonie and I were out the back of his place, sharing a beer. Boonie's Augusta hideaway was so far away from anything I'd ever experienced before. We sat under a huge spreading tree overlooking a vast inlet where flocks of waterbirds and flotillas of small boats puttered and pottered around in the ebbing sunlight. It was magnificent, and in spite of the tense rage I felt over my board, I was unwinding. I hadn't realised the toll the last few months had taken on me.

Boonie being a straight up Aussie classic helped a lot. He was cruisy and laid back, completely relaxed about everything, and yet seemingly on top of everything. He had a gorgeous home in a spectacular part of the world, an old but well decked out four wheel drive, a small but robust fishing boat, and a loving, funny, family around him.

"Yeah, I reckon he's moved on," said Boonie. "Not just out of Margarets, but out of the south west altogether – maybe even the state, or the country."

"How's that?" I asked.

"Well he said he had a job to do. Reckoned it might take him…what'd he say? 'Far and wide', that's right. So he could be anywhere by now."

"Thanks Boonie," I said, draining the last of my beer. "I've taken enough of your time, I'll be off."

"What's the rush?" said Boonie. "You sure as shit won't catch him tonight. Where're you gonna you stay?"

"I'll drive back to Perth and wait for a flight home," I said. I had a mission – and the notion that the thief wasn't some desperado dole bludger but a man with a job that took him around the world only strengthened my resolve. He had no reason to steal my board, he could obviously afford his own; it was an act of bloody-minded cruelty.

"Bullshit," said Boonie flatly. "You'll stay here overnight, we'll go for a surf in the morning. There's a beaut point break I reckon will be on not too far away. Somewhere special. Hardly anyone knows about it. We'll take a run out there tomorrow. You won't regret it."

"But work. My board," I protested. "Another email might show up tomorrow."

"They expecting you at work tomorrow?"

"No, I've briefed them that I may be away for some time."

"Well I'll give you the wifi password and you can check your email any time. I've got a board you can use, and a wet-suit. All the charts say the point'll be crankin' tomorrow. And if it is, it'll blow your mind."

I couldn't disagree. The beer was so tasty, the environment so serene and inviting, and the idea of surfing a special spot so irresistible that I nodded, and he laughed. He was excited.

So Boonie and his wife Wendy and his kids Tommy and Eva and I had a barbecue and a few more beers, and I slept in their spare room. At five am, Boonie woke me, and we set off in the dark, nursing cups of coffee on our laps, with boards, dogs and God knows what-all in the back of his four wheel drive ute.

For forty-five minutes we dodged kangaroos and the other assorted wildlife that criss-crossed the road in front of us as the arriving sun lit the clouds up. At first they were tinged with darkest purple, then flaming orange, and then at last, as the blazing disc itself crested the horizon, brilliant, fluffy white. Turning off road in the growing light, we spent almost an hour on a jolting, hilly, boggy, sandy track that took in farmland, forest, and finally sand dunes. Tall trees crowded the track, big, burly roos kept on jumping out of the shadows and bounding down the track in front of us, all muscles and bravado, and the air smelled fresh and clean and dewy.

We emerged on a huge sand and black rock point covered with green-grey coastal scrub that struggled to get above waist height. Boonie swung left and took off down another hellish track across the point. Fifteen minutes later we were standing at the top of a hundred-metre precipice, looking down on an oily smooth ocean. I was reminded of an endless pane of ridged glass.

Long, snake-like columns of swell marched across the still sea to explode on deserted beach breaks as far as the eye could see, each facing a sandy ochre-coloured cliff. At the bottom of the steep incline in front of us, solid black-green waves pounded rhythmically onto big, round black rocks of old lava, careening swiftly down the point in a peeling right-hander.

Boonie had showed me a map – the point simply sticks out into the ocean like it was placed in this endless series of bays for the sheer pleasure of trapping swell, a billion years ago. There wasn't a human being to be seen, and as the car park looked to hold a maximum of around six vehicles, we wouldn't be expecting a crowd.

We unpacked and picked our way down the cliff as quickly as possible. I was nervous. On unfamiliar territory in a strange place on a surf trip that was uncomfortably unstructured for someone like me, with a man I'd met only twenty-four hours before. But Boonie seemed genuine enough, and his joy at the sight of that magnificently ragged coast with its incredibly well ordered swell lines was real enough to infect me. I might have been scared, but I was exhilarated.

Boonie got into his steamer and I got into the short armed

steamer he'd loaned me, happy that the fit was fairly close. Then we walked across the rocks to the obviously critical jump-off point, and waited for a break in the white water. Standing there with Boonie's wetsuit on, one of his boards under my arm and one of his dogs standing casually by my side, I again started to feel a long way from my office and my home – my comfort zone I guess you'd call it – and I struggled not to let my nerve fail. The waves looked pretty big down here at water level – easily well over six foot on the sets, maybe more – it was hard to judge.

Suddenly Boonie yelled, "Go!" He leapt into the water and started paddling furiously. I had no time to hesitate – I threw myself into it and followed him, scrambling over a rising wave with the dogs barking wild encouragement from the rocks. For the next three hours, Boonie and I surfed alone.

The takeoff varied from easy, fat slides to jacking vertical drops, and either way it scooted you into a warping bowl over a shallow section of black rocks that often threw square. If you made it through there alive, you'd run a cross a semi-fat section where you just had time to ride up to a high line to set up for a true screamer – a booming hollow wall. You couldn't afford to slow down too much for the barrel though, because when you exited the hole you had to be going Mach 3 just to make the next stage, also generously round and hollow, before getting the hell out of there as the whole lot unloaded onto a too shallow ledge.

Boonie talked me through every section and guided me through every manoeuvre I should make, until I was making almost every wave – after a few sobering drubbings, of course. It was frightening, being that isolated and copping tonnes of cold, hard water on the head, not knowing which way was up. But after a couple of character building wipeouts that I survived quite well, I gained confidence and started to enjoy it.

Boonie spoke a lot about this ancient coast, how it had formed and why these tall cliffs stood with their toes in the water, and his fears for its future thanks to an expanding population and growing knowledge of the break we were on. I spoke to him of my work and life, and although he didn't really say anything, I got the impression he thought I was a bloody idiot for spending all my time locked in offices and meetings when I didn't have to work at all.

"It's all got to do with being driven," I said a little defensively. He just laughed.

"Don't worry mate, I'm driven too – to enjoy meself, and to ride as many of these sweet south coast waves as possible in my short time on earth." He called me into a wave, and I took it, revelling in the weird, almost unknown sense of freedom I was experiencing.

Later, we sat on the rocks and ate tuna straight out of the can, then chilled out for an hour before going back in the water. After an hour or so of that marvellous mechanical perfection, I was spent, and I paddled in. Boonie stayed out there another hour and a half, and I watched him tearing the point apart. I envied his control and his obviously intimate knowledge of the wave, and the thought struck me that whilst he didn't have all the money and accoutrements that I have, his was undeniably a very rich life.

Late that afternoon, we pulled into Boonie's driveway, and it didn't take much for him to convince me to stay another night. We cracked a can, fired up the barbie and sat under his big tree, eating, drinking and telling Wendy about the waves of the day. Much later, in a haze of beer and exhaustion, I started getting cranky about my thief again, insisting that I would find him and visit cruel justice upon him.

"You really ought to relax more, man," said Boonie smiling. "Hurting him won't fix the hurt you feel. But if it makes you feel any better, I think he said his job would take him somewhere in Indonesia – some island or other. Maybe you ought to follow." I said I would consider it, and Boonie added, still grinning, "Sounds like his job's a lot more fun than yours, doesn't it?"

"Yeah, I suppose it does," I said.

Next day I thanked Boonie and Wendy, briefly offended them by offering them money, and left with a promise that I would come back again soon and surf the point with Boonie on my Microchip board.

That night in a hotel room in Perth I checked my email and found a new message, from the skipper of a charter boat in Indonesia. He had both my Microchip and my thief on board, and would be docking at Padang, Sumatra in three days. I replied to say that I would be there when the boat arrived.

I caught a flight home, spent the next day in my office preparing my staff for my extended absence, and packed. After the Boonie experience, I figured that wherever I went in search of my board, I'd take enough surf gear to make use of the waves I was almost bound to find. I reasoned that I may have time to kill in the quest, and that I may as well sharpen up my surfing skills for when I got my board back. The image of Boonie being so totally at ease – at one really – with the waves at the point had driven me to desire the same for myself.

Standing on the hot, humid dock in Padang, I watched seven deeply tanned, mangled, deliriously happy surfers disembark from the charter boat Barrel-Time. All of the boards that came off the boat were in covers, but none of the surfers closely resembled the man Boonie had described, so I hurried up the gangplank and found the skipper – a big, brawny Aussie with shoulder length bleached blonde hair and a slow, relaxed grin.

"Yeah the guy – put his name in the log as Jim Smith – jumped ship on a tiny island about eight hours steaming time from here. Could've gone island hopping any which way from there. The Mentawai Islands is a long chain, and from there you've got the Banyaks and the Telos, so it's a pretty big playground. Great bloke but. Fantastic surfer, really cool dude, everyone loved having him on board, eh. Told a lot of great stories, made everyone feel, I dunno, as though they were his best mate."

"Yeah, well that great bloke stole my board," I said testily. "Did he say anything about a job he had, and where that might be?"

"Yeah, he talked about some kind of job he needed to do, or that he was on or something. Kind of mysterious about it really, but definitely mentioned it. Couldn't tell you where but."

I tried to chill, but I was feeling pretty dejected about it. I'd wasted my time. He studied me for a minute, and then he seemed to have an idea. Almost as if that asshole who'd stolen my board had inspired him.

"Listen," he said. "The next charter is a ten days from now. I was going to give the cook and deckie a little time off and go for a bit of a cruise meself. I could use a hand occasionally, and you look like you need a holiday. You wanna come? I'll charge you fuel and food only, and we can call it a private charter.

We'll get a few waves, take in a few spots, and you can look for your board thief."

I'd told my staff that I'd be away for some time, so I agreed. Next day, after refuelling and reprovisioning, we set sail.

I can't describe the time I spent with Skipper Tom in enough detail. There aren't enough adjectives, and nowhere near enough superlatives, but if there were I could fill all the pages in the universe with the story of that one short week.

We surfed, it seemed like hundreds or even millions of deserted breaks on vicious, vibrant Indonesian reefs beneath clear crystal waters. We barrelled backhand and forehand. In offshore breezes beneath blazing sun, in deadly calm under dull grey skies, off atolls and islands and bommies, we surfed and we saw.

Sunsets and sunrises, moondances and starlights shone down upon us smiling, chilling, enjoying. We charted no course, watched no clocks – we just went wherever and whenever we felt like it, and we scored the best waves of my lifetime.

Of course, I couldn't shake my desire to find my thief, so at those few places where we surfed with others else I quizzed them. To Tom's bemusement, I spent hours out of the water scouring dusty villages and empty spaces searching for the man who always seemed to be just one jump ahead of us.

On a couple of occasions we ran into other charter boat operators, friends of Tom's, and they told us, yep, they'd seen a bloke on a Microchip board, surfing harder, deeper and faster than even the most experienced Indo vets.

They all said the same thing – don't know where he went or what he might be doing now, but mentioned he had a job to go to. That was it.

Every day I used Starlink to check my email, and for my trouble got nothing but business bullshit. I left most of them unanswered.

In spite of the fact that I was feeling and surfing the best I had for years – probably ever – the need to find the thief gnawed at me. Tom found it all hugely amusing.

"Mate, we've got Bintang and barrels, and no one to give us the shits – why in the world would you have the shits on? Just give yourself a rest for gawd's sake."

Of course, he was right, and I began to suspect that I was learning to enjoy myself at long last, but I still had my mission.

All too soon, our odyssey was over, and we were steaming to Padang to pick up Tom's next charter. I sat on the bow of his boat, watching the impossibly blue water slip away below me like time, and wondered what to do next. I really didn't feel like going back to work, but in the absence of anything else to fill my time, I was thinking, "Why not?"

But then, I thought that if I just went back to work, I may never find my board, and worse, that all the time I'd spent on looking for it would have taught me nothing. I went below to pack all my stuff, as we were nearing port, and checked my email. I was expecting just business correspondence and nothing more.

I couldn't believe it when I opened up the email server, and there was a message from an old school friend, Griff. The last I'd seen of Griff, he was eking out a living shaping boards back home, and as work and ambition had gotten the better of me, I hadn't seen or heard of him for years.

His email told me what he'd been up to. Still shaping, but now in Mundaka, Spain, and working in the local surf shop.

Of course, I'd heard of Mundaka – probably the most famous hard core rivermouth left in the world, and my initial thought was "Good onya Griff – way to make a life for yourself!"

But then I got excited, because he wanted to let me know that for the last few days, a hombre named Jim had been blowing everybody's mind in Mundaka. Taking on insane, thick, huge barrels and playing them like an old fiddle, like he'd been doing it all his life.

This Jim was riding – of course – a Microchip board, and making even the most gruesome triple overhead drops look like fun. Griff apologised for not getting in touch sooner, but he'd only seen my ad on a swell chart site that day, and got onto me immediately.

Tom pulled into the smelly harbour in Padang, and before I walked away from Barrel-Time I gave him a big bear hug – probably my first ever – and told him what a brilliant, life changing experience our trip together had been. He laughed, and said, "Yeah mate, I don't run an enterprise like yours, but somehow I don't care. Best of luck, eh."

I took a flight from Padang to Kuala Lumpur to make the long journey to Spain. I had to wait two days for a flight to Madrid, and I took the time to walk around a city once more, finding new joy in the colours, chaos and scents of an Asian capital after a ten idyllic days of sea, surf and isolation. Oddly, not once did I sit and fret about my company or my work, or whether I was being irresponsible for not being there to run an outfit that was really big enough and well staffed enough to run itself.

The flight from KL to Madrid was a long one, followed by a short hop to Bilbao, where I hired a car, then drove the sixty kilometres to Mundaka. The little town sits, or rather squats, on a green hillside with the cold Bay of Biscay spreading out before it, and the wide river mouth stretching across a vast sand bar. Just off the coast, there's an angular island, on which you can see long lines of breaking waves running all the way along it, with a tiny monastery perched atop the craggy hill near one end.

As I drove the twisting road from the nearby fishing town of Bermeo, my first glimpse of Mundaka was of a small church sitting defiantly on a pad of green right on the point, and I felt an almost religious certainty that I would be reunited with my board here and my quest would be at an end.

Griff and I sat outside the Bar El Puerto, which presides over the town's tiny harbour, and sipped on a *cerveza*. Beyond the sea wall, just a hundred metres away, Mundaka was doing its thing – serving up big green barrels to an armada of wet-suited surfers.

"I heard you were a workaholic," he said with characteristic directness, drawling through every word. "Thought you'd given up surfing for more serious stuff."

"Yeah, I almost had Griff," I told him, "And I have to admit, my idea of surfing has changed a lot in the last couple of weeks. I might've kept up my surfing through these years, but I've been what I suppose you'd call a corporate surfer. Now I'm just a surfer who owns a corporation. As soon as I get my board back, I'm going to live the way I always should have. So tell me that the guy's still here, that he hasn't gone off to do this fucking mysterious job."

"Hah! Sorry mate," grinned Griff. "I spoke to him out in the lineup the other day. Big, mackin' barrels steamin' through and the tide was ripping out, so it was pretty edgy stuff, and there were only a few of us taking it on. He said he'd almost finished his job – whatever it is – and that he'd be leaving Mundaka in a couple of days. Saw him out there yesterday, and I reckon he bailed this morning."

"Shit! I've missed him again!" I snorted. "I can't believe it!"

"Well maybe not," said Griff. "He said that when the job's done, he's coming back. Could be a couple of days, could be a couple of weeks."

"If that's the case mate, I'm staying right here. I can wait for the bastard, no problems."

"Yeah cool," said Griff. "I can find you a flat somewhere in town no problems, or you can even stay here at the El Puerto, rich bloke like you. But I would say one thing mate," and he looked at me with unusual gravity. "When his job's done and Jim comes back, don't be surprised if you can't be too pissed at him any more."

"No chance of that," I retorted. "The wanker pinched my board and took me on a chase half way around the world!"

"Exactly," said Griff with a sly smile.

Over the next two weeks, I lived in a room right above the little port, waking up each morning to the most glorious view you can imagine. Straight out my window, the peak of the Mundaka sand bar stood up and started its long ride to the other side of the river six hundred metres away, almost always breaking in flawless symmetry.

The break itself is capricious, difficult to learn and hard on back-handers. Bitterly cold ice-melt from the Pyrenees flows swiftly down the river on the outgoing tide, meeting powerful Atlantic swells on a surprisingly hard sand bar. Sometimes just staying on the peak is a challenge, the water moves so quickly.

When it's decent – which was almost every day of that fortnight, the takeoff is hard and fast, steep as a mountain side. The time I'd spent in Indonesia had sharpened my skills and I took to Mundaka with genuine confidence, revelling in the achievement when I made it. From the takeoff, there's a jacking section that demands a high line and some fast footwork that sets up an awesome wide-mouthed barrel, and I plucked some of the finest tubes of my life there. I found that I no longer analysed and criticised every wave – I simply took it as it was, and thoroughly, deeply enjoyed it.

When I wasn't surfing, I plunged into the local lifestyle – staying up late, wandering from bar to bar with Griff and his wife and friends, chatting, drinking laughing, arguing loudly. I even started to pick up a few words in Basque, the local language, and found many very alluring Basque girls who were willing to acquaint me with their native tongue.

I doubt that I've ever been happier, and I've definitely never been less concerned about what I should be doing other than enjoying my life.

One night after a typically late dinner, I met Griff and his wife Arantxa in the Bar El Puerto, and after a couple of *cañas*, we walked around the corner to the Portubide, a compact, smoky little bar on the edge of the town square. We walked in there and Griff and I fronted the bar for a couple of *vino tintos*. "You've been pretty quiet about Jim the last few days," said Griff.

"Yeah," I shrugged. "I guess I'm a bit over it now mate," I said. "When that mongrel lifted my board, I was pretty pissed off. And I promised myself I'd go find him, and get my board back. But the process of finding him has changed me I guess. Don't get me wrong, I'd love to get my Microchip board back. But in a lot of ways, his act of thievery has done me a lot of favours, so I don't suppose it's worth me getting aggro about it. The only one it affects is me, in the end."

"I'm glad you said that," said Griff. "Because there's someone here I want you to meet." He stepped back, and there stood Jim – as described to me by Boonie, Tom and Griff – holding out his hand. I was instantly a taut, angry, vengeful person – and then I wasn't. It passed.

I shook Jim's hand, and felt the distinctive warmth of another human being. My hatred evaporated, and my quest dissolved. He looked me squarely in the eyes and said, "listen Scott, I think it's time you got your board back. I've taken good care of it, it's completely undamaged – in fact it goes like a shower of shit. I'll bring it around to Griff's tomorrow. They say the swell's picking up, you should be able to ride it at all-time Mundaka."

I nodded dumbly.

"I'm sorry I had to take your board mate," he said simply. "But it was my job."

"What job?" I asked.

"Doesn't matter," he said. "It's done."

The Burnt Islands

Night filling in a supermarket is hard, repetitive, and insanely boring. Stacking countless boxes, jars, cans, packets, bottles, sachets, tubes, rolls and sundry other over-packaged items that nobody really needs, on grimy shelves spotted with rodent shit, hour after mind-bending hour. But at least night filling keeps you out of the pub and delivers a regular paycheck. Money you can save to realise your dreams. And that's all I cared about – all I thought about – those long, tedious nights.

Until the day came when I'd saved enough. Invested enough time and effort lugging cartons, mindlessly picking, moving, stacking clear racking, ensuring that every label was pointed in the right direction, to earn myself the surf trip of a lifetime.

No three weeks in Bali for me. I booked passage on a cargo ship steaming through the Indian Ocean to Sri Lanka. From there I planned to make my way around the world, hopping from surf spot to blazing, pumping surf spot, with enough cash to keep me travelling for a year or more and enough nous to score work on the way.

By Christ I was happy the day I told the boss to take his braised steak and beans and stick them up his chocolate aisle. I packed my boards and surf gear, threw in a few pairs of shorts and a couple of singlets, kissed mum goodbye, awkwardly hugged my brother, and stepped aboard the *Tamil Tiger*.

Brown, dirty water issued from the bilge of the rusty old cargo slut as we slipped away from the wharf at Fremantle. I stood at the railing of the ship and waved, calling out goodbyes to the fishermen watching the departure, and then we were underway. On board were a crew of twelve, myself and one other passenger – an ancient lady who was heading to Sri Lanka to reunite with her family.

We left Freo harbour as the sun sank, a giant golden orb behind Rottnest Island. Overhead, the vivid clouds put on a spectral show, and the coast of Western Australia disappeared behind us. I sat on the bow of the ship and said goodbye to my past. The sky turned orange, then faded to pink, deepened to a heavy maroon and finally dimmed to black. Watching it I drank my bottle of duty free bourbon. I crashed early and slept the sleep of the just.

By morning we were surrounded by sea, nothing but blue, rolling swells from horizon to horizon, alone but for the never ceasing hum of the massive diesel engines below decks and the occasional escort of leaping, happy dolphins. The food I ate with the crew was fine, if a little spicy, and as the day wore on I got a bit lonely, suffering a tinge of regret at completely abandoning my former life. But I was glad to be going adventuring, and as I strolled the deck, I foresaw nothing but positives. On we steamed, through classically clear conditions, appearing to make no progress on the endless blue we were crossing, but always getting closer to my destiny.

Late in the afternoon of the second day, I was in my cabin, desperately looking for something to fill in the time while the hours dragged tediously by. The endless vista of the sea rolling by had finally lost its fascination, and my iPod wasn't cutting it. I began to wish I'd spent more time selecting my playlists, because out there, Spotify was a distant memory.

I dug deep into the recesses of my backpack, feeling around for the book I'd stashed for just such an occasion, realising that if I'd already gotten desperate enough to read something, the future could be bleak.

Suddenly there was a dull **boom** from deep in the bowels of the vessel, and I was thrown across the cabin as the boat heaved over on its side. Almost instantly I was thrown back across the tiny room as the hull righted itself, overcorrecting. I grabbed hold of the bunk as the whole vessel rocked back and forth like an oversized pendulum for a full thirty seconds, before finally settling enough for me to stand up again.

There was silence for a brief half second, then alarms started going off everywhere, and I could hear running and shouting. The voices were panicked, and the fear rose in my throat like a block of cement. I could hardly breathe. A crewman ran past my cabin, stopping only long enough to bash on the door and scream, 'abandon ship'.

That's when the terror took me. But I discovered that even in such an extreme situation, though I was inwardly petrified my actions were calm, deliberate and calculated.

With shaking hands but rugged determination, I grabbed my backpack and boards, and man-handled the whole bulky package out of the cabin, up the narrow passageway, climbed the stairs and emerged on deck. As I did so, another explosion rattled the vessel from top to bottom, and muffled screams could be heard from somewhere down there. The Tiger started to list badly and the stern was beginning to sink. I didn't have much time. Hurling the boards and backpack over the rail on the low side, I jumped in after them.

The shock of being in the water was hideous. Luckily it wasn't cold, as we were up near the equator, but the reality that I was floating in the wide Indian Ocean, possibly thousands of miles from the nearest land, hit me like a shark bite. Still, I managed to hold it together and do what needed to be done.

I took the boards out of the two double board bags I'd brought with me, chucked the bags and lashed the four boards together with leg ropes. Thankfully I'd brought a full quiver with me, against all the advice of my mates back home.

Once the raft was completed, I took off the heavy backpack, which had made swimming a bitch but which I was not prepared to lose, and tied it in the centre of the board-pontoon. This was a lengthy process, and by the time it was done I was exhausted.

At last, I had time to look back at the Tamil Tiger. She was drifting away from me and sinking quite quickly now, and then in an almighty gulp, the blackening sea swallowed her whole. I didn't see anyone jump from the ship as she went down, nor could I see or hear another soul in the water with me. I don't know if the crew all stayed on board because they couldn't swim or whether they'd all been killed or trapped, but it seemed I was wholly and inconsolably alone.

I wondered about the tiny old Sri Lankan lady who'd been heading home to see her family. She probably never made it out of her cabin.

The tropical night fell with brutal finality, and I floated, close to tears, through the starry open ocean night. Without the need to act to survive, which had proved a fine distraction, my calmness evaporated and blank horror embraced me.

Terror isn't something I'd been too well acquainted with before, but that night I became thoroughly familiar with its every evil aspect, painfully aware of its every shade and tone as the darkness swallowed me and I was engulfed in despair. I lay across my boards, sobbing and occasionally wailing as unknown beasts splashed and swirled around me, and the quiet lapping of the waves bored into my brain.

I was absolutely certain that I was going to die that night, and I must confess I didn't face it serenely or with resignation. I decided that if anything attacked or came near me, I'd fight tooth and nail, and if necessary scream like a baby to scare it off. But that wasn't courage, it was a cowardly desire to ensure that I would piss the attacking beast off, so that if I was going to die it would be quick.

Tensed ready for action, I waited for the silent death that didn't come, and almost fainted from joy as well as exhaustion when a thin green line of light split the sky from the ocean in the predawn, and the night was over. It was only then, when I knew that the darkness was behind me for at least another twelve hours, that I slept. As I drifted off, I almost smiled as I thought that I'd been given the adventure I craved.

Sleep was fitful, and disturbing dreams scudded across my mind like shadows across the sun, until the rising heat of the day bathed me in a clinging film of sweat and I could no longer endure it. I sat up bolt upright on my raft, and wiped the stinging salt sweat from my eyes.

The sun was high now, blasting a million shards of hard light from the ocean into my eyes, making them water.

'Don't!' I cried to myself as the tears streamed down my cheeks. 'I need those tears, they're the only water I have.' But I lost my tears, and never had further cause to lament their passing, because when my vision cleared, I saw an island.

It was a low, old island fringed with a reef and laced by a dirty sand beach, and behind that a number of small, round, bald hillocks speckled with small outcrops of distant greenery. There were a couple of other smaller islands flanking the big one, ancient coral atolls that have become true islands, with scrubby vegetation and the odd palm tree; flashes of life and colour.

They weren't good looking islands of the sort that you'd see in tourist photos. Rather, they were brown and sort of scorched looking. Vaguely forbidding. Of course, to me, they were the most beautiful sight I'd ever seen, and I wept again in relief at being saved.

Wearily, I forced my arms to paddle my cumbersome raft towards the shore, where the deserted whitish-coloured beach was half hidden behind a line of foaming breakers.

'Jesus!' I thought, 'I've got my boards and stuff here – maybe I'll even get a surf!' But this was a random phantasm brought on by delirium, and I dismissed it to focus on getting ashore, and hopefully getting some water and food into me. I needed to find out where the hell I was, and how I was going to get away from there.

A little more than twenty minutes later I was dragging my assemblage of boards and backpack across the sand, having taken a fairly severe working in the healthy swell pounding the reef not far from the beach where I'd landed.

Fully spent, starving and dehydrated, and feeling more than a little Robinson Crusoe-ish, I lay down on the warm sand in the shade of the fringing coconut palms, and quickly fell into a kind of semi-coma.

I don't know how much later it was that I awoke, but when I did I found that I was in a soft, comfortable bed in a cool, dark room. I tried to sit up, but a big hand stopped me, and a booming voice said, 'Don't try to move. You've had a difficult time and you were close to death when you were brought here. Just relax.'

'Where am I?' I managed to croak out.

'These are The Burnt Islands, and you're safe here, so just relax. We will go outside and have a little *faka*, and you get some rest, *eyah*? '

As my eyes adjusted to the dimness in the room, I could see that the resonant voice belonged to a big, dark man, and that there were a couple of other people in the room with him, a heavy woman about the same age as the man, and a young girl who I guessed to be their daughter. Even in the dusky gloom I could see that she was incredibly beautiful, with flawless skin and wide, onyx eyes.

The three of them, who had clearly been sitting some sort of vigil over me, got up and wordlessly walked out of the room. I was still in a state of nervous exhaustion from my ordeal, and struggling to cope with the idea of waking up among these people on their 'Burnt Islands', so I closed my eyes and drifted off into another sleep.

The next time I woke up, I was being watched by the lovely young female, and from the deepness of the darkness I could tell it was night time outside. I struggled up onto my elbow and looked at the girl, seeing only a shadowy outline in the dim light – faint but enough to show me the fine curve of her neck and the regal pose in which she sat, silent. Not too far away, I could hear the crash of waves, deep and hollow in the quiet of the night.

'Wow!' I said, almost to myself. The girl looked up at the noise, and I stared at her through the blackness. 'I don't know about you, but this is freaking me out!' I said to her.

Out of the darkness came a voice soft and low, entrancing in its velvet gravity. 'You are the first visitor to these shores in over forty years. The people of the Burnt Islands are "freaking out" about you just as much as you are about them.'

The delicacy of her deep, clipped but quite English accent almost allayed my disquiet at what she was saying, but I understood that these people who had saved me and cared for me were not sure about whether I posed a threat to them. Was I merely the scout – the first in an endless stream of wreckers come to destroy their culture and their harmony?

The fact that they'd left this young girl to watch over me meant that they probably didn't think I was too dangerous on my own, and that was something.

She lit an oil lamp, and in its gentle golden glow there shined sweet serenity in her depthless obsidian eyes. A winning smile played on her perfect lips, and her entire being radiated a positive energy and calmness I'd never known could exist.

'Hey, I'm completely in your hands here,' I said. 'I've just jumped off a sinking ship in the middle of the Indian Ocean, and I don't mean you people any harm. Just give me a couple of days to recover my strength and *phhhht*, I'm out of here! But thank you for your kindness,' I added as an afterthought.

The smile she gave me to indicate that she understood was dazzling, but she stayed silent, and got up and walked out of the hut. When she came back she was carrying a big bowl of steaming broth, which I wolfed down hungrily, thinking that maybe everything would be all right.

The girl watched intently as I ate, and after a few mouthfuls I felt obliged to try and chat with her. Partly because the sight of her simply watching the food go into my gullet embarrassed me, partly because she made no effort to start a conversation, and mostly because I was dying to get to know her.

'My name's Marco,' I told her. She flashed me that vivid smile again and said, 'How do you do, Marco, I am Maha-Li.'

'Very pleased to meet you Maha-Li,' I replied, and held out my hand, which she took in a soft, warm and lightly moist hand, and shook with tender strength.

'I come from Australia. Have you heard of it?' Realising how stupid the question sounded, I quickly backpedalled. 'I mean, if no one's been here for forty years. . .'

But Maha-Li smiled, taking it all in without altering her placid expression. 'We know a little of the outside world, but only as much as we care to know,' she began.

'We Burnt Islanders have been here since time began, and never felt need for contact with the outside world. We were content to tend our *faka* crops and celebrate our *faka* religion, and never set foot off our islands except to fish.

'In those times, our home was known as the Green Isles. But several generations ago, people with white skin like yours arrived. British people who called themselves missionaries. They told us not to celebrate our religion, and raged against our ritual and daily use of the *faka* we grew as evil. They taught us the language we now speak, and tried to deter us from our religious practices, which are based around the *faka*, but we were strong in our resolve.

'The *faka* has been good to us since the world first turned, teaching us much about ourselves, and we refused to bow to their demands. Then one day without warning, many large British aeroplanes arrived, filling our skies, making our grounds shake and darkening the day, spreading fear and, then, death and desolation, crushing our souls.

'A man came and told us, "the British Cotton Company has agreed with the government that the weed you call *faka* is evil and wrong, and you will not grow it any longer." How the people of the Green Isles laughed.

'"The *faka* is good," they said. "It makes rope and material for clothing and housing, the oil from its seeds is nutritious and healing, and the flowers when smoked impart a serenity of mind and a clarity of the soul. It is the basis of our very beliefs! We cannot and will not stop growing the *faka*." But the Britishers would not listen. With their planes they sprayed our Islands with a foul chemical that seared and scarred the land, and within just a few weeks, almost all of the *faka*, which had covered these islands for countless centuries, died.

The missionaries, fearful of succumbing to the famine their friends had caused, all disappeared then and never came back, leaving our Green Isles as the Burnt Islands you see now. They were difficult, tragic times for the people of the Green Isles, and many died. But we survived, and we now call our lands the Burnt Islands so we never forget what was done to us.'

'That's an incredible story,' I said to Maha-Li, 'and I hope you don't think I'm being rude, but I feel kind of light headed now, and I think I need to go back to sleep.'

She laughed, a short, rich chuckle, and grinned broadly at me, flashing perfectly straight white teeth. 'Of course, there are still many pockets where the chemicals did not penetrate, which allowed us to continue to grow *faka*. Today much of the land has recovered from the injury that the chemical did it, and we are at last expanding our crops. There is some *faka* in the broth I gave you, and that is making you light-headed.'

I lay back and soaked it all into my now buzzing head. 'What these people call "*faka*" is obviously weed!' I thought, almost giddy at the idea. 'Holy Shit! I've stumbled on The Garden of Eden, Utopia and El Dorado all at once…' And with these happy thoughts bouncing around in my mind, I drifted off to sleep.

When I awoke it was daylight outside, warming up nicely in the room I was in, and I felt fabulous. Almost as soon as I was awake, Maha-Li appeared with another bowl of broth, which I again wolfed down.

The breakfast brew was obviously quite lightly spiced with *faka*, because rather than feel buzzed and out of it, as I had the previous night, I felt only calmed and empowered by its warmth. Feeling pretty strong, I insisted on getting up and exploring these Burnt Islands that were once the Green Isles.

Maha-Li seemed to accept without question that she was my guide and protector, and she ushered me out of the hut into a sensationally sunny, balmy day. I saw her in the bright light of day for the first time, and I was again astonished at her tranquil beauty. Her face was shaped like a perfect almond, her skin glowing dark amber, her lips full and her cheeks flawlessly rounded. She was easily the most attractive woman I've ever seen, and I've never met anyone who could match her for exquisite loveliness and deep inner and outer peacefulness. Suffering my rude examination in proud silence, Maha-Li spread her arms and indicated the land around us, drawing my attention away from her magnetic self.

The low hills of the Islands sure looked brown and burnt, but looking more closely I could see that there were quite a few tiny patches of green here and there where the *faka* was being grown.

'We have established some new gardens for the *faka* now,' said Maha-Li, 'but we will never again devote our entire island chain to its growth, even though we consider growing *faka* to be our sacred duty. We understand that to make our Burnt Islands green again would be to invite the terrible British and their chemicals back. And the next time, I am sure, we would be utterly destroyed.'

As we walked, Maha-Li introduced me to the people of the Burnt Islands. The first people I met, I recognised from the previous day; her father, Bulu-Ka, who was the Chief *Faka* Grower, and her mother Maga-Li who in this matriarchal society was considered the mother of the whole island chain. As a guest of the matriarch, I was accorded much respect and friendship from everyone that Maha-Li introduced me to. And whenever we met anyone, or stopped to chat, we were offered *faka*.

We smoked it in funny little bong type set ups made of coconut shells, we ate it in seaweed patties (sounds disgusting, tastes fantastic), we sucked on little pipes, and we smeared a wicked green-brown oil from the *faka* on fishcakes and ate those. By the time we'd made a circuit of the big island I was completely stoned, practically a dribbling mess and in need of a good lie down, and Maha-Li looked as fresh as she had that morning. Clearly this *faka* took some getting used to.

I had a little nap, and at about dusk Maha-Li came and led me to a feast in my honour. She had obviously explained to her people that I wasn't some spy for the British, and that I had no means of getting off the Islands or communicating with the outside world, so they were ready to accept me as one of their own.

They bestowed me with the name Marco-Ka (-Ka being the suffix for 'man', -Li being the suffix for woman, every-one had a -Ka or a -Li attached to their name – though I'm sure you've worked that out already), and we all got completely bombed on the finest pot I've ever had the privilege of smoking and ingesting in my life.

It wasn't like the pot I'd furtively smoked with my brother our and friends back home; this was a gently mellow, opening and sharing experience. It made one feel in touch with himself and with everyone else, and it made the air smell clearer, the stars shine brighter, and the heart beat stronger. There was dancing and singing, tons of seafood and fresh vegies, and of course *faka* from here to breakfast-time. I have no idea what time it was when I staggered off to bed.

The next day I awoke in my own hut, with my boards and stuff neatly stacked in one corner, and once again Maha-Li came in with a big bowl of the *faka* broth for breakfast. And there began the most blissful period of my entire life.

Like everyone else on the Islands I was expected to help with fishing or tend the *faka* gardens for a few hours a day, but there was plenty of time off, most of which the Islanders spent in contemplation of the *faka*, unravelling its mysteries and 'learning their own souls', as Maha-Li put it.

The Islands were blessed with a number of good surf breaks, so I put in a good couple of hours in the water every day, much to the delight and amusement of the Burnt Islanders who watched.

As time passed, I began to be properly initiated into the rites and beliefs of the *faka* religion of the people. I learned much about the herb; its healing and preventative properties, its strength and durability when woven, how to cook with it while chanting the sacred mantra, and how to open my mind more and more each time I ingested it.

The *faka* helped me to discover my own fears and weaknesses, to meet myself in my own mind and be comfortable with the person I met there. The people of the Burnt Islands were the most relaxed, pacific and generous people I have ever encountered, and I'm certain that their *faka* religion was the source of their placidity. So I consumed and studied it with great gusto, hoping to become as self aware and as composed as them.

The people, for their part, accepted me very naturally and I was able to offer a few horticultural tips that the people hadn't thought of, which led to the development of an even stronger strain of the *faka* than they already had. In a few short months I was truly a part of the society, and had almost forgotten my previous existence. Best of all, though, was that my friendship with Maha-Li blossomed, and we spent a lot of time together.

Maga-Li, Maha-Li's mother and the matriarch of the Burnt

Islands, looked kindly on our growing friendship, and her father Bulu-Ka and I fished together, worked together, and explored our *faka* souls in many, many sessions together. All was right with the world.

One of the few males the same age as Maha-Li and me, and certainly the coolest of them, was Turu-Ka, and he quickly became a great mate too. As are all of his people, Turu-Ka was amazingly open and friendly, and we smoked and ate a fair bit of the *faka* together. He didn't seem to mind my attachment to Maha-Li, even though it was plain to everyone on the Islands that he was practically dying of love for her.

One day over a few pipes of *faka* oil, Turu-Ka asked me if I'd teach him to surf. At that point, I was getting kind of sick of surfing these fantastic waves by myself (who in the world could ever say that?) so I agreed. I took Turu-Ka out onto the reef just in front of the main beach, and being the handy kind of island guy he was, he picked it up pretty quickly. Within a few weeks he was charging the outer reefs with me, surfing cavernous barrels as casually as you like, and we encouraged each other into bigger and meatier waves.

I was amazed that Turu-Ka had picked up surfing so easily and quickly, but then he was a superb swimmer, handled a canoe in any kind of seas with ease, and had no fear of the reef or the waves. This was unusual in the Burnt Islanders – most of them considered the sea to be full of harsh spirits, and they only went out in the open ocean when they had to, sticking to the lagoons and staying close to shore when they went fishing.

The three of us – Turu-Ka, Maha-Li and myself, soon became practically inseparable, hanging out, fishing, working in the garden and getting into *faka* meditation together. The *faka* religion was opening my eyes to my own self daily, and I was really becoming a Burnt Islander in my own mind. I'm not sure at what point it happened, but somewhere along the line I determined never to go back to what is laughingly termed 'civilisation'.

One typically sunny, swell-ridden offshore kind of day, I came in from a solo surf – Turu-Ka had been nowhere to be seen in the morning – and as I walked up to my hut, I could see that there was some kind of a party happening over at Maga-Li's central hut.

I dumped my board and had a quick *faka*, then wandered over to Maga-Li's place. By that time I'd seen enough to know what was going on – it was a birthday. Maha-Li's birthday.

The people of the Islands still forgot to specially inform me some of their more important celebrations, which everyone seemed to know about without a word being spoken, so I wasn't terribly miffed about not getting an invite. I knew that if I simply walked in there would be no drama. The hut was always open, and I walked into the fire-lit gloom with a smile on my face.

There in the centre of the circle of villagers sat Maha-Li in a stunning gown of flowers and garlands over a weave of the finest, softest *faka* hemp, and when she saw me enter she smiled so sweetly and lovingly that I almost melted. The hum of the gathered crowd halted the moment I walked in the door, and the people parted to allow Maga-Li to turn her maternal gaze upon me.

'Ah, Marco-Ka. You have decided to accept our invitation after all...' she started.

'What invitation?' I asked, puzzled. All eyes turned towards Turu-Ka, most none too kindly. Maga-Li held up a hand to quell the buzz that had started among the crowd, and silence again fell at once. Maga-Li spoke again.

'Turu-Ka was supposed to have informed you. It is a great sadness to me that he has not – he is not in touch with his *faka* soul, and wishes to avoid contest through cowardice.'

The crowd murmured approval, Turu-Ka glared at me in shame, and I thought I saw anger in his eyes – the first time I'd seen any sign of such an emotion in the Islanders.

'Today we come together to celebrate Maha-Li's nineteenth birthday,' Maga-Li continued, addressing the crowd at large now. 'And as tradition commands, it is time for her to choose a mate. A man whose loins will provide the fruit for her womb and ensure that the Mother of the Burnt Islands is a woman of strength and calmness. For one day, Maha-Li's daughter will be Mother of the Islands, as will Maha-Li when I am gone.' The reverent hush that cloaked the room was almost tangible.

'Until a short time ago, Turu-Ka was the only eligible male on these Islands with the strength of *faka* and the tranquility of soul to mate with Maha-Li. Now the newcomer Marco-Ka, who has become one of us, is also eligible. As he has helped us create a new and stronger *faka* with his outworldly knowledge, so too might his blood mingle with ours to strengthen our line. Particularly as it seems that Turu-Ka has lost the *faka* strength to face his own jealousies and fears.'

Maga-Li said all this with the customary equanimity of the Islanders, but the weight of her words was unmistakable.

At first I thought I'd had too big a pipe before I'd come into the hut, but it soon dawned on me that this was for real. I was being put up as a potential candidate to be Maha-Li's husband and one day take over as Chief *Faka* Grower. I looked solemnly at Maga-Li and bowed my head, then turned slightly to smile in Maha-Li's direction.

I caught sight of Turu-Ka's face burning with shame and embarrassment as I did so, and averted my eyes. Now, this was the first time in my months on the Islands that the words 'jealousy', 'fear' or 'contest' had ever arisen, and I was a bit stunned about the whole deal. I began to feel as though my presence had upset the equilibrium of the Islands, and that trouble would come of it.

Especially when Maga-Li looked at Turu-Ka and said, 'Turu-Ka, you shall be the one to choose the form of contest.'

Later, Maha-Li told me that on the odd occasion that these things had arisen, the usual thing to do was have some kind of *faka* based contest – eat it, smoke it, whatever, and whoever was still standing at the end wins the right to be the girl's mate. But Turu-Ka stunned me, Maha-Li and everyone else when he looked me in the eye with his old, *faka*-based calm, and said, 'Surf contest.'

The whole hut hummed with excitement as the people realised the situation, and Maga-Li looked more than a bit unhappy when she said, 'Never before has such a contest been entered upon. But Turu-Ka has made his choice. The contest will take place in two days.'

As I walked away from Maga-Li's hut a couple of hours and a psychedelic mixture of different forms of *faka* later, Turu-Ka caught up with me and we walked together. He was anxious, apologetic and, typically, deferential. He said that he hadn't really known what had come over him back there in the hut. He had experienced true jealousy for the first time in his life, and it had spawned a feeling of anger, another emotion he was unused to. It frightened and shamed him that he didn't have the *faka* soul to control it.

He kept on apologising to me, and even offered to back out of the contest, to let me win by forfeit, but I wouldn't hear of it. I told him I was not worthy of being his opponent, that he was the better man for Maha-Li and for the Burnt Islands, and it probably would have been better for all if I had never arrived on their shores.

He accepted my words with humility, but reiterated what Maga-Li had said about my coming being a boon for the Islands, and bringing the possibility of strengthening their bloodline. We parted outside my hut best of friends, as always.

Later, when Maha-Li told me that a *faka* contest was the standard approach, I realised how much his anger had cost Turu-Ka. In neglecting to tell me about the celebration, he had failed his *faka* soul, and his decision to nominate a surfing contest was his attempt to atone for his loss of courage and his surrender to negative emotions.

He knew, of course, that in a smoking contest he would have whipped me properly, but in a surf contest I would have a definite edge. That one moment of raw frustration had more than likely cost him his chance to be Maha-Li's consort and the Chief *Faka* Grower.

It was a mark of the man that in true *faka* style he'd come to terms with his own failure and redeemed himself by giving me the advantage.

Poor Maha-Li was almost beside herself, in her calm and poised way. That such an extraordinary event could arise out of our fast three-way friendship was amazing and terribly regrettable to her, but there was nothing any of us could do; the die was cast.

The three of us hung out together constantly over the next couple of days, and our friendship was stronger than ever – probably because we knew that one way or another our relationship was about to change. We made the most of our remaining time as one person with three distinct facets.

The day of the contest dawned in a spray of pink and purple clouds, and a gentle breeze buffed a solid ten foot swell – easily the biggest yet I'd seen it. The break by the local beach was unrideable at that size, so the contest was to be held out on a reef on the other side of the island, a massive ledging, tubing left that we'd christened *Faka-lana* – meaning *faka* waters.

The entire village piled into canoes and rafts, and the fleet travelled the calm lagoon circling the island, parking as a giant flotilla in the channel beside *Faka-lana*.

Both Turu-Ka and I were nervous about the contest – the surf was thick and huge, the tide was sketchily low, and the crowd was really psyched. They'd never contemplated a contest like this before, and most of the Islanders actually avoided the area, so it was a massive occasion, with heaps of *faka* oil fish- and seaweed-cakes being handed around, and laughter rising in great clouds from the armada.

Turu-Ka and I were on Maga-Li's floating platform, and she was to be the judge. Beside her sat Maha-Li, as radiantly beautiful as ever I'd seen her, but almost as nervous as Turu -Ka and me. Poor Maha-Li knew that only one of us could win, and already her heart was breaking for the other. Or so it seemed to me when I saw her smile mournfully at both of us.

We drank a ceremonial cup of lightly *faka*-laced coconut milk, and went for the boards. Turu-Ka was tall and heavy, so I let him take my 7'6", while I grabbed my 7'2". We paddled across the channel and into the peak easily enough, wishing each other good luck as we did so.

On the peak, there was no time for talk – massive swells were pushing through with alarming regularity, thundering to a hollow, booming death on the coral just a couple of feet below the surface.

Almost as soon as we got to the take-off spot, Turu-Ka turned and paddled and kicked into a hulking eight foot beast, disappearing in a shower of spray and foam. From the screams of delight echoing from the channel, he'd obviously scored a monster tube, and he rocketed out the other end to stab into a gouging re-entry, the spray of which shot off the back of the wave like a geyser as I watched.

A bigger wave loomed, and I turned and paddled. The drop was incredible – as steep as the mountain trail to the highest *faka* gardens, as fast and treacherous as the vipers that lurked in the shadows; like nothing I'd ever seen before, let alone ridden. The lip, impossibly thick but perfectly shaped, threw over me in a wide arc, enclosing me in a tube like a crystal ballroom, glittering with the colours reflected off the razor-like reef below.

I held a high line through the tube, and as it settled a bit, I spread my arms as wide as I could without coming even close to touching either side. The crowd in the channel went wild, and as I was spat out of the tube I set up for a vicious round cutback, and pulled out of it just in time to duck into a second tube, which sent the crowd completely ballistic.

For almost two hours we charged the waves at *Faka-lana* like men possessed. Turu-Ka was fearless, pulling into loads of late drops and making them, ripping through huge cutbacks and intense re-entries, and casually, confidently riding through barrels like glass caverns. At one point he even pulled off a seriously risky floater on a wave with a face about two stories high.

The swell kept on jacking, and by the time we'd been there for an hour and a half, the sets were over twelve foot, maybe more. The reef was becoming lethal, just about maxing out, and the tide was at the bottom, so the coral was mere inches from our fins as we negotiated the boiling trough of each wave.

A blistering set wave rolled towards us, and both Turu-Ka and I paddled for it, him on the inside. As it jacked, it went beyond vertical, and I looked down to see the reef almost sucking dry.

I pulled out, fully expecting Turu-Ka to do the same, but to my disbelief he jumped to his feet and took a straight drop down the most frightening face I've ever seen. As he disappeared behind the wave, I heard the crowd collectively 'ooh', then 'ahhh', and finally a boisterous shout of triumph – Turu-Ka had made the wave, and I could tell from the way the crowd was reacting that the contest was won.

Maga-Li held up a flame-red cloth to signal that it was over, and Turu-Ka and I paddled across the channel together, exhausted, elated and thunderously applauded by the Islanders. I can honestly say that it was the best surf, the best feeling, the greatest day of my life. Even when we stood on Maga-Li's raft and she solemnly threw a big, green *faka* branch glistening with resin at Turu-Ka's feet to declare that he'd won, I couldn't be disappointed.

Once again, thanks to the Burnt Islanders, I'd learned something new about myself. And I had a new level of respect for Turu-Ka and his incredible courage. He'd been ready to die to win Maha-Li, and he deserved his victory.

Back on the Island, a two day feast was thrown to mark what was widely regarded as the finest moment in the history of the Burnt Islands, a day when the spirit of the people finally met the spirit of the water that surrounded and gave them life, and understood it.

Of course, Turu-Ka was over the moon — his incredible skill and courage in those awesome waves had made him the toast of the Islands — but to his credit he was more interested in congratulating and commiserating with me than he was in being the winner.

Except when he saw Maha-Li emerge from her mother's hut in a gorgeous floral marriage costume. Then he was almost overcome by the emotion of the moment, and leaned on me for support, which I gladly gave him.

At any other time and place in my life, I would have been bitter and twisted about the result — but the *faka* religion had shown me my place in the world, and I was content to kiss Maha-Li lightly as she approached, and formally hand her over to Turu-Ka.

A few days later, with the reluctant blessing of Maga-Li and Bulu-Ka, and against the impassioned protests of my dear friends Maha-Li and Turu-Ka, I boarded a long canoe loaded with provisions and a mountain of *faka*, and paddled away from the Burnt Islands.

Although I loved the life there, I felt that I loved Maha-Li too much to see her with my best friend Turu-Ka every day. I felt that I should leave the Burnt Islands to the Burnt Islanders and return to my own people.

Heading south and east as I was told, I found myself on the beach somewhere in the northwest of Australia about a week later, and dragged my canoe up onto the sand.

I was very comfortable with the idea of living off the land and the ocean by then, so I buried my *faka* and started hiking and hitch-hiking south. Within a week I was back in Perth, trying to get over the grief I felt at losing the love of my life, my best friend and a lifestyle the rest of the world can only ever fantasise about.

My family was thrilled to see me – they'd believed that I was dead for over a year. But after the excitement of the reunion, every one went back to living their lives, and I felt terribly alone. And I knew I couldn't go back to stacking supermarket shelves.

I headed back up north and retrieved the *faka*, taking it south to sell. I believed – like a bloody fool – that I could spread the wisdom and peace of *faka* religion as I sold it off in one ounce lots. But by the time it was all gone I realised that the smokers back in 'civilisation' were only looking for escape, not enlightenment. I was seen as some kind of nutter when I started talking passionately about the *faka* religion.

With the money I made from the Burnt Islanders' generous gift of *faka*, I bought a yacht, and I've been sailing the Indian Ocean, searching for the Burnt Islands, for a couple of years now. I simply sail around, fishing, smoking the *faka* that I grow in a special cupboard on board, and meditating on my *faka* soul.

I keep searching for the Islands because I know now that I should have stayed. My *faka* soul would have continued to grow strong with the Burnt Islanders, and I would still enjoy the love and friendship of Maha-Li and Turu-Ka, which I have never known from anyone else.

Because I was foolish enough to believe that if I couldn't have it all I wanted none of it, I lost everything that was important to me and my *faka* soul.

I know in my heart that I'll never find the Burnt Islands, because no man leaves paradise and finds it again.

About the Author

Nick Bruechle is an Australian surfer, writer, and slave to a blue heeler named Munty. He has spent over 45 years in the advertising industry, loves to travel, and is married to the most wonderful woman in the world, Rachel.

Connect with Nick via:
Facebook: @nickbruechlebooks
Twitter: nick_bruechle
Email: nick@nickbruechle.com

Also by Nick Bruechle:
The Psyman
The Reprint
The World Without Mirrors
The Cat Man